FaraWay FroM HOMe

Lara Hunter

ISBN-13: 978-1533598097

ISBN-10: 1533598096

DEDICATION

To Megan and Heinie.
Thank you for being such beautiful people and great friends to
my daughter. You are loved!

CONTENTS

ACKNOWLEDGMENTS

Cassidy-Jane, your contributions and wild imagination help keep me on track. You are a smart girl with so many talents – one of them being my muse. Without your clever thoughts this book would not be possible. Thank you.

1
ALL ABOARD

The sun beamed through Sarah's bedroom curtains. She lay on her bed looking through the new Geography book her parents had got her for school. It was filled with pictures, maps and famous explorers. There were pictures of beautiful mountains, wild animals and far-away lands. The Explorers were born hundreds of years ago with long beards and funny names. They came from all over the world. Sarah was so lost in the book that she barely heard her mum calling her.

"Sarah, it's a lovely day outside. Why don't you go and play with your brothers in the garden?"

Sarah sighed. It was not as much fun playing with her baby brothers because they were so small and she had to watch them all the time. She climbed off her bed and called back to her mum.

"Yes, Mum. Mikey. Chris. Let's go and jump on the trampoline," she continued calling as she headed out of her room and into the lounge.

The two boys came running around the corner screaming with excitement as they chased each other. Sarah had to jump out of the way before Chris could run into the back of her.

"Come on," she said, grabbing Chris around the waist and picking him up as she headed for the back door.

Mikey ran after them.

"Me too. Me too!"

He bounced around her trying to get her to pick him up too.

"I can't carry both of you, Mikey. Wait until we get outside."

Sarah lifted Chris onto the trampoline and then bent down and picked Mikey up, placing him on the trampoline too. The boys immediately started to bounce around. Sarah climbed on and started jumping with them but her mind had already started to drift off. Imagine...

"Allll aboard," Rick hollowed from the deck of the boat.

He was wearing his favourite farmers hat. It was wide brimmed, floppy and made of straw, with a leather strap around his chin. He also had a large navy blue puffed jacket on. He waved his arms at the girls to signal that they should come onto the boat. Sarah grabbed Maggie's hand and pulled her towards the ramp.

"I hope we have everything we need," she said.

"We can double check now before we leave," Maggie replied as she followed Sarah up the ramp.

"Rick, can we do one more check? I really want to make sure we have everything we need," Sarah asked Rick, once they were on the deck.

"You girls worry too much. It will be fine. Let's go."
Sarah knew that Rick was itching to get the large boat out onto the open waters.

"No, Rick. Sarah is right. We have a long way to go and we have to make sure we are prepared," Maggie said, as she headed for the hatch.
Rick sighed and followed the girls below deck.
Maggie and Sarah were the best of friends and did everything together. Maggie was a kind, thoughtful person with a playful nature. Rick, Maggie's oldest brother had decided the girls needed a man on board to take care of them. He had invited himself to join them. Both girls were happy he had come along. After all he had designed and built the boat himself. Rick loved to tinker with things and was really good

with his hands – he had a smart brain too. He was fun and mischievous but always looked out for the girls just like a big brother would.

All three friends headed down the long, thin passage that led to a dark store room at the bottom of the boat.

"I'll check the equipment. You girls check the food and water supplies," Rick instructed.

Sarah had made the checklist weeks before and handed each of them a copy. Rick took his and headed for the far corner where all the equipment was stored. Sarah and Maggie began ticking off the list of foods in front of them.

After what felt like hours, Rick declared,

"Everything is here!"

"Yip, we have everything here too," said Maggie.

"Okay, let's do this then!" Rick exclaimed with excitement, as he raced up the open ladder and onto the main deck once more.

He ran towards the upper deck, climbed the few steps that led to the boat controls and started the engines. The motors roared to life and the water at the back of the boat began to bubble from the force of the propeller as it spun.

The girls leaned over the railing, watching as the boat moved slowly, away from the dock.

"Here we go!" squealed Sarah with excitement, as she squeezed Maggie's arm.

"I'm feeling a little nervous," Maggie admitted.

"Me too!" Sarah responded, as she placed her arm around her friends' neck.

"But it is going to be so much fun. Can you believe we are actually doing this? We are going to discover unexplored land!"

"Let's hope we can actually find it," Maggie said, frowning at the thought of them getting hopelessly lost.

The two girls stood watching as the dock got further away and the people got smaller.

"Soon we won't be able to see land. That's such a scary thought," Sarah said, starting to feel even more nervous than before.

"Too late now. We are on our way, girls!" Rick said from behind them. Both girls jumped.

"Shouldn't you be steering the boat?" Maggie said, pushing at her brother's shoulder.

"Go back up there and do your thing!" Rick laughed and walked off and back up to the upper deck.

"Can someone bring me a map so I can set the GPS, please. Don't want to get lost now!" he teased, raising his eyebrows at the girls.

Sarah went below deck and collected the map, a compass and a bag of chips.

The three friends sat on the lounger, on the upper deck and studied the map. Happily, they munching away at the bag of chips. Then Rick jumped up. He began steering the boat towards the centre of the harbour walls, that led them out into open waters.

Three hours later the land they had left behind was just a speck in the distance. The boat was on auto pilot and it sailed slowly in the direction Rick had set the GPS.

"Who wants to play checkers?" Maggie asked.

"Yeah, that sounds like a good idea. When are we going to start dinner though? I am starving," said Rick.

"You are always hungry. I'll get the checkers while you two decide what we are having for dinner."

Maggie disappeared below deck.

"Steak!" Rick exclaimed, with enthusiasm.

"That's all you ever eat. Meat!" Sarah said, rolling her eyes.

"We have to make sure we eat healthy food so we don't get sick out here, remember?"

"Yes, Yes.." Rick said, sticking his tongue out at the thought of greens.

Maggie reappeared from below with the board game and began setting it up on the wooden table, that was built into the main deck.

"So what did we decide on for dinner?" Maggie asked, looking up at the other two.

"Your brother wants steak. Are you going to cook it?" Sarah turned to Rick with a grin on her face.

"Sure, right after I beat you both at checkers!" He exclaimed, sitting down at the table.

The three friends played happily for some time. Rick kept winning and the girls were getting frustrated. Until, Sarah caught Rick sneaking an extra marble into his territory on the board.

"No wonder you keep winning. You cheat," exclaimed Sarah, punching Rick on the arm. Both girls jumped up and attacked Rick. They jumped on him and playfully pretended to beat him. Rick just laughed and pretended to be helpless to their attack. The girls were laughing too as they backed away from him and stood with their hands on their hips expecting an apology.

"Okay enough checkers," Rick said, finally.

"I am going to cook."

"Yes, I think that is a good idea. Do something useful," Maggie commented, brushing her hair over her shoulder and pointing in the direction of the hull.

Rick just laughed at her. He disappeared below deck leaving the girls to pack the game away.

Suddenly the boat began to sway, rocking wildly from side to side. Maggie dived for the marbles that were now rolling off the table and all over the deck.

"What's going on?" Sarah shouted.

"I don't know but..." Maggie began but was interrupted by a loud noise that sounded like a volcano exploding.

"RICK," both girls screamed at once.

Rick was already running up from the hull, as he had also felt the boat swaying, while trying to cook their food in the kitchen. He ran straight to the railing and looked over and into the water.

Not too far from them was a pod of whales frolicking in the water. Holding the railing firmly they watched as the whales played about.

"Did you know that whales are one of the most intelligent creatures in the water? If a mum dies then another female in the pod will feed and take care of the baby," said Sarah, matter-of-factly.

Both Rick and Maggie had turned and were staring at her.

"What? I love animals."

She shrugged.

"You know that?" said Sarah, turning to Maggie.

She smiled at her friend and leaned over the railing again to watch the whales.

Neither Rick nor Maggie said a word. They just turned back to the water, impressed with the knowledge Sarah had about whales.

But Rick, being Rick, could not leave it there...

"So Miss Know-it-all, what type of whales are those?" he asked, tilting his head towards the water.

Sarah continued to watch the whales playing around in the water, rocking the boat with the force of their tails as they rose and fell, creating waves that quickly reached the boat, swaying then back and forth.

"I think those are humpback whales. Do you see the grooves from under his chin?" asked Sarah, but didn't wait for anyone to answer.

"That is so they can open their mouths really wide to take loads of fish in one gulp."

"Cool," said Rick.

Maggie nodded her head with interest. Just then one of the larger whales swam directly under their boat. The waves the whale created sent the boat rocking roughly from side to side. He came out the other end, swam a small distance from the boat and then seemed to rise out of the water. The whale dived and his large tail hit the water creating a huge splash which wet the three spectators on the boat. The girls screamed with delight. Rick jumped back trying to avoid the mass of water that sprayed up and over them. He brushed the water from his clothes and ran his hands through his hair. Shaking his hands off, to rid himself of the excess water, he muttered under his voice.

"Ah, man. I am soaked."

The girls, who were also dripping wet, turned to see a very unimpressed Rick. They started laughing at him while jumping about trying to shake the water from their own bodies.

"Scared of a little water, hmm?" Maggie teased her brother.

"Very funny," Rick smirked.

"I'm going to change and finish dinner. Tell your whale friend to keep it down out here so I don't burn the food."

Maggie and Sarah just laughed and turned back to the water. In all the excitement they had not realised that the whales had moved on.

"Ah, they are going away," moaned Sarah, watching the whales drift off into the distance.

"Come on, let's finish packing this game away and then go and get ourselves dry," said Maggie, sympathetically.

She knew how much her friend loved animals.

The girls picked up all the marbles they could find, packed the game away and headed down into the hull for a shower. When they returned to the deck, Rick was putting out some knives and forks.

"Do you need any help?" asked Sarah.

"Nope. Thanks, I've got it sorted. Be back in a jiff with the food."

The girls sat down and looked out over the ocean. The sun was setting and the view was breath-taking. The water had turned to a smooth, black silky rumpled sheet and the sky was a mixture of orange, red and greys. A thin layer of clouds lay at the horizon and cut the sun through the middle creating beams of light streaking through the top and peeking through the bottom.

"Wow, that is amazing," said Maggie.

"Mmm," was all Sarah could reply.

"Earth to girls?"

Rick broke the silence. He placed three plates of food on the table and sat down with the girls. He looked up for a brief moment, picked up his knife and fork and dug into his steak.

"Eat up, it's getting cold," said Rick, without lifting his head.

Sarah picked up her knife and fork without looking down – she did not want to miss a minute of this amazing sunset. Rick, who seemed unfazed by the view, continued talking.

"We should make the island within the next three days, all going well."

Nobody answered so he continued.

"I was thinking, if we turned the boat around now, we could be back home for breakfast."

Sarah was the first to respond.

"Home, why are we going home?" she asked.

"What?" said Maggie.

"Just checking that I am not talking to myself," Rick said, grinning.

"But I do think we need to plan out the next three days and what we are going to do once we hit land," said Rick.
The girls said nothing, as they thought about what Rick had said.

"So I was thinking..." He paused for effect.
Both girls just looked at him. So he went on.

"When we get to land we should only take the few things we need, from the boat, until we know what is on the island?" he tilted his head, waiting for the girls to answer.

"That's seems fair. What did you have in mind?" asked Sarah.
Rick pulled out a pen and paper and started making a list. The girls gave suggestions and by the time dinner was over they were happy with the list they had put together.

"Let's put this to one side in the storage room tomorrow so we can make sure we have everything,' said Maggie.

"Good idea. I am stuffed. Does anyone want something to drink?" asked Rick.

"Me, please," said Maggie.

"Me too, please," said Sarah.

Rick piled the three plates on top of each other and disappeared below. He returned with three cups of juice and shared them out.

"I'm going to my bunk to study the map. The boat is set on course so nothing to worry about. Night girls," Rick said, glugging down the rest of his juice and vanished below deck, again.

"Night," the girls answered as he closed the door behind him.

"I think I am also going to bed. You?" said Maggie.

"Um. I am tired," said Sarah, standing up and following Maggie below.

Lara Hunter

2
ROCK THE BOAT

Sarah woke up as her body hit the floor. The boat was rocking wildly from side to side. She had been thrown from her bed. Her elbow hurt. She reached up to her arm and began rubbing it but the motion of the boat rolled her to the other side of the room and she hit her head. Sarah felt panic rising in her stomach as she reached for the bump on her head.

What was going on? She thought.

Everything was dark but she could hear the wind ripping at the sides of the boat. As the water moved around the outside of the boat, it sounded like they were in a water tunnel. The water seemed to surround them completely. Sarah reached out to grab anything she could find. Her hand touched the wall. She crawled closer, lifted herself up and used the wall to steady herself to her feet. Slowly, keeping her back to the wall, she crept towards the door and flung it open. In the distance she could hear Rick shouting. The wind kept steeling his words and Sarah could not make out what he was saying. She moved slowly, in the direction of Rick's voice. She heard her bedroom door slam behind her and jumped in fright. Everything was dark. Sarah used her hands and body to slide against the passage wall, as she made her way towards Rick's room. Thump. Sarah walked right into the closed door in front of her.

"Ow," she moaned, close to tears.

"Rick, are you in there?" she shouted.

"YES! The handle broken the side," was all Sarah heard.

Sarah turned the door handle and the door flew open as the boat tipped to one side. Sarah was flung into the room and crashed straight into Rick.

"AAAAW," they yelled at the same time. Rick grabbed Sarah by the arms.

"Are you okay?" he asked, as they stumbled a few steps to the left, then back to the right.

"Yes, but where is Maggie?" said Sarah, her voice trembling.

"I don't know. I have been stuck in here, since the storm woke me," he said.

"The storm?" asked Sarah, confused.

"Yeah, there is a massive storm outside. I have no idea what shape the boat is in but I need to take a look. Can you find Maggie?" asked Rick, squeezing Sarah's arms to give her courage.

Sarah just shook her head as Rick pushed past her and headed back into the passage. Sarah turned to follow him, swaying from one side of the passage to the other. She found Maggie's door and flung it open.

"Maggie?" called Sarah, squinting her eyes to search the room for her friend.

"Aaah."

A soft moan came from the corner of the room. Sarah quickly moved towards the sound.

"Maggie?"

"Here," said Maggie softly.

Sarah got down on her knees and crept along the ground. The boat continued to rock, making it difficult for Sarah to move, straight forward, towards Maggie. When she was close enough, she reached out and touched Maggie, gently.

"Where are you hurt?" asked Sarah.

"Aaaah," moaned Maggie again.

Sarah felt helpless and frustrated. She could just make out Maggie's body on the ground but she could not see anything else. She moved closer and touched Maggie's head. She stroked her hair softly and asked again.

"Where does it hurt, Maggie?"

"My head," Maggie mumbled.

Sarah ran her hand, slowly and gently, over Maggie's head. Suddenly her hand felt warm and wet. She knew it was blood. Sarah thought quickly about her next move. *'Where was the first aid kit and a torch?'* She thought.

"I'll be back as soon as I can. Don't try to move," she instructed Maggie, and left the room, as quickly as the rocking boat would allow.

Sarah was rocked around as she headed down to the kitchen and storage room. She almost fell down the steps but managed to hang onto the railing and keep herself on her feet. She took a minute, so her eyes could adjust to the darkness of the storage room, before trying to reach the far corner. There she would find the first aid kit. The boat tilted violently and she fell to her knees. Too afraid to get up, she crawled over to the far wall. She grabbed the first aid kit and then looked around for the crate that would have a torch. Still on her knees, she moved towards the crate. She search through the box and found two torches. She checked for batteries, grabbed a bag from the box, shoved everything inside and made her way back to the stairs. She began to wonder what had happened to Rick but knew she had to get back to Maggie. A head injury was serious and Maggie should not be left alone for too long.

When Sarah got to Maggie she was moaning loudly.

"What's it? I'm here. It's gonna be okay," said Sarah trying to keep her friend calm.

"Oooow," Maggie cried.

"My head really hurts."

"I got you. Just lie still," said Sarah as calmly as possible, though her hands were shaking.

"I need you to sit up. Are you hurt anywhere else? Wiggle everything carefully," Sarah told Maggie.

Maggie moaned again but did as Sarah had asked.

"Nothing else hurts," said Maggie, lifting her head.

Sarah gently placed her hand under her arm and helped Maggie to sit up. Maggie moaned with every move but managed to sit up. Sarah shone the torch over Maggie's head. Maggie squinted at the bright light. Sarah found the gash at the back of Maggie's head. Carefully she mopped up the blood around the wound. Once it was clean she studied it carefully to see how deep the cut was.

"It doesn't look too deep. I think your head is just really sore from the sudden bump. I can bandage it up for you," said Sarah, as she unpacked the first aid box, in search of a bandage.

Carefully, Sarah applied a cream to the cut and then closed it up. Just as she was finishing up Rick came down the passage, yelling for them.

"We're here," shouted Sarah, above the blasting wind and waves that still beat against the boat.

Rick came through the door and went white when he saw his sister.

"Oh, no, what happened? Are you okay? What can I do?" Rick stammered, checking his sister's head and then the rest of her body.

"I'm fine Rick, thanks to Sarah," said Maggie, more cheerful than she had been since Sarah found her.

"Good," he said to his sister and then turned to Sarah, "Thank you."

"It's all good. What's happening out side?" asked Sarah.

"It's a massive storm but I have managed to secure everything. There's not much we can do now but wait out the storm," he said, shrugging and sat down next to his sister. He put his arm around her and she leaned her head on his shoulder. Sarah moved in next to Maggie. The friends sat quietly as the boat rocked, listening to the noises coming from just outside the boat, as the sea raged and the wind pounded on the water and the boat.

3
LAND

Rick was the first to wake. Everything was quiet and the boat was still. Carefully he reached for a pillow. As he slid away from Maggie, he gently lay her down onto the pillow. Tiptoeing, he crept up to the main deck. The sun shone brightly, the water was a smooth sheet of glass and he could hear birds singing.

"We made it. We are here," shouted Rick, as he ran below deck to get the girls.

"Wake up, wake up. We have hit land," Rick yelled with excitement.

Sarah jerked awake, confused.

"What's going on?" she asked.

"Land. We have found land," said Rick, almost jumping about with excitement.

"Land?" asked Sarah, still a little confused. Then suddenly she opened her eyes wide, jumped up and ran to the port hole. She looked out and around.

"Where?" she asked, even more confused.

"On the other side," said Rick, laughing.

"Oh."

Sarah ran to the other side.

"Land!" she yelled.

"Maggie? Maggie?" whispered Rick, gently nudging her.

Maggie stirred and then slowly lifted her head. She groaned and grabbed her head.

"Slowly," Rick moved closer and helped her up. "We have found land, Maggie," he whispered to her.

"Really? Is the storm over?" she asked.

"Yes. Come on. I'll help you up to the deck," said Rick, taking his sisters arm.

Sarah, Maggie and Rick Stood at the railing and starred at the view in front of them.

To either side of them was a long, wide stretch of glorious, golden sand that seemed to sparkle in the morning sun.

Directly in front of them was a thick, green blur of palm trees and bushes, sprinkled with colourful flowers and berries.

The bush looked untouched. There seemed to be no pathways leading into the forest as the trees and bushes zig-zagged through and twisted around each other.

Rick helped Maggie to the store room and together the three friends, carefully, packed all the goods they would need on land, for now. Packing it into the small row boat, they had brought with. Maggie climbed in first, followed by Sarah and then Rick. Once they were all settled, Rick lowered the boat and rowed them to shore.

Rick was beaming as he dropped the large black crate he was carrying onto the sand. He shook his arms and stretched them out. They hurt from the weight of the crate he had been carrying, but he was too happy to care.

He walked back to the water's edge. Stopping, he looked across the ocean that lay calmly, with just the gentle sound of the small waves that rolled onto the beach and back into the massive pool of water, from where it had come.

Again, he bent over the small rubber boat, bobbing on the water and tugged at another crate that needed to be carried to shore. He lifted it up with a groan and carried it over to the first crate.

"Come on girls, we have work to do. The sun is not going to shine all day and we still have to build a shelter before sunset."

The girls turned and looked at Rick as if in a trance.

Slowly Sarah walked back to the boat and grabbed a canvas bag in each hand. She placed them beside the crates, still not saying a word.

Maggie followed close behind with the last wooden box that was on the boat.

"Are you okay?" said Rick, watching the two girls.

The girls stopped and looked up at the vast green smudge of thick bush in front of them.

"Yip," said Maggie, finally. "I just can't believe we are here."

"Yeah, me neither," said Sarah, letting out a long breath.

"Hey, relax. We have been planning this for ages. We have everything we need and if we can just get our shelter set up today, then we can start exploring tomorrow," said Rick.

"Okay," said the girls, at the same time, sounding a little more excited.

Rick looked around the beach.

"There!" he pointed at a section of the beach that lay the furthest away from the water.

There were a few, large but smooth rocks and some fallen trees on the edge of the forest.

He picked up the black crate and began carrying it towards the spot he had pointed to, as he spoke.

"This will be perfect for our hideout. It seems more sheltered and we can use these fallen trees to build our shelter."

The girls each picked up an item and followed Rick without saying a word.

Once they had moved all their gear to the new camp site Maggie finally spoke.

"What do you need me to do?"

"Maggie, could you start collecting some small rocks, sticks and twigs for our fire. Sarah, you can help me move these broken trees onto the sand so I can clean them up," said Rick.

"Sure," said Maggie and wondered off along the edge of the forest to see what she could find.

"How many trees do you think we will need?" asked Sarah.

"We need to make the shelter big enough for the three of us and all our stuff. If we make it too big we may not get it finished before sunset. So," Rick picked up a stick and began drawing lines in the sand.

"If you lie down in there, then I can get an idea."

Sarah did as he said. She lay down at the one end of the rectangle on the sand.

"Now roll over three times."

Sarah rolled over and stopped after her third roll.

"Right, so we can put the crates and box here," Rick continued, as he mapped them out in the sand and completed the rectangle.

"There," he said.

"Now we need to measure the trees and see how long they need to be and how many we will need."

He strolled over to the crate and scratched about. Finally, he pulled out a tape measure and a small saw. Then returned to the poles and began working. They worked tirelessly for a few hours.

"My tummy is grumbling. I need to eat something," said Sarah, almost to herself.

Rick glanced up at the sun. It was sitting just above the horizon like an enormous yellow ball.

"We are nearly done. Soon there won't be much light and we need to finish," said Rick, pleadingly.

"Okay," said Sarah, as she tied the last wooden poles together with weaved flax, that they had gathered.

Maggie returned with her last armful of small twigs, her hands clutched some medium sized stones and her pockets with sagging with larger ones. She dropped everything to the ground and emptied her pockets, then dropped to the ground, exhausted from carrying her heavy load. Carefully, she made a circle with the rocks and stacked some twigs and thicker pieces of wood in the middle. She then piled the remaining wood on one side.

"Maggie, can you please help me?" asked Rick.

Maggie got up and went over to her brother. Together they hoisted the poles up and onto the roof of the shelter. Sarah ran to the other end, reached up and stopped it in line with the other poles, already in place. She then tied more flax around the poles to join them together. Rick climbed onto the roof. Maggie past him the large palm leaves. He spread them evenly at first, and then placed more on top, facing in the opposite direction.

"Right, now some rocks," Rick shouted, down to the girls.

Lying on his tummy, Rick reached down and took the small boulders, one by one. He placed them all around the palm leaves. It was important to make sure there were no gaps for the rain to come in, plus, the boulders would

keep the leaves from blowing away. Once he was certain they had done enough to keep the roof on their shelter, he climbed down.
Standing back he looked at their new home.

"Pretty good for a bunch of kids, ay?" Rick laughed.

"I think it's awesome," said Sarah, excited.

"We rock," said Maggie moving to stand inside of the little room. She reached up to touch the ceiling but it was too high.

"Let's get all the gear inside and then we can sort out dinner," said Rick.

"Good idea. I am starving," said Sarah, relieved to be closer to eating, as her tummy growled loudly. She wrapped her arms around her middle and giggled. "I am really hungry."
They all laughed as they carried their things into the little covered space. The walls were made of upright poles, slightly apart and filled with a covering of palm leaves. It kept the wind out but allowed a little light to peep through the gaps.
Rick went over to the pile of large stones and twigs that Maggie had carefully put in place. He made a shallow moat in the sand, between the wood and rocks, then cleared away any stray leaves or twigs. He placed a few smaller

stones directly around the pile of wood, in the centre. These would get warm from the fire and keep the heat in longer. Carefully he re-arranged the wood in a tepee-like shape with the small twigs underneath. They had brought matches with but these would not last forever, so he had to make sure the fire lit the first time round.

Crouching down, as close to the wood as he could get, being careful not to burn his nose, he struck the first match. It flared and then died out. Rick sighed with frustration. He lit the second and cupped his free hand around the end of the match. The match flared and started to burn. Moving slowly, he placed the match up against a dry twig. The flame died. Rick grunted.

"Here try some of this newspaper. Maybe it will help!" said Maggie, standing over him with a slight grin on her face.

"I forgot we brought that," said Rick taking the paper from her.

"Thanks."

This time he lit the paper and placed it into the pit beneath the wood. The twigs started to crackle as the flames caught them. The paper quickly wrinkled and became ash. Rick fanned the small flames, gently. Then, as they all watched, not daring to breath, the twigs began to burn, one by one. Some of the bark on the larger pieces of wood caught light. Maggie and Sarah came and sat down around the small fire. They all watched as each piece of wood caught alight and began to turn black, with orange and yellow flames dancing above it.

"So, what are we eating?" asked Rick, breaking the silence.

"I have taken out some baked beans, sausage and bread," said Sarah.

"Sounds good. Is it ready to go on?" asked Rick.

"Yip, I will cut the sausage into the pot with the beans so we don't have to dirty too many dishes. I hate washing dishes," said Sarah, rolling her eyes.

"I don't mind doing the dishes. Maybe we can all take turns, then nobody has to do it all the time?" suggested Maggie.

"I can live with that," said Sarah, smiling at her best friend. She was always such a thoughtful person.

By the time the dinner dishes had been cleaned and packed away, the sun had disappeared, leaving the sky black with only the twinkle of tiny stars, dotting the heavens above them. The air was cooler. Replacing their shorts with sweat pants and adding their sweat tops and jackets on top, the three friends went back to sit around the fire. The fire crackled, little sparks jumped off the wood while the flames rose high above the burning wood. Rick added more wood to the fire, while they studied the night sky and horizon in front of them. It was so peaceful but eerie at the same time.

Were they completely alone on this island, thought Sarah, *or was someone stealing a peak through the trees?*

4
"WHAT WAS THAT?"

Rick had made the fire close enough to the shelter so the heat would move through and keep them warm into the night but safe enough that the wood of the shelter could not catch fire. They each climbed into a sleeping bag, ready to settle down for the night. Sarah lay in the dark staring up at the roof. She could hear the waves crashing on the beach outside. A gentle breeze made a soft swishing noise through the trees behind her.

Suddenly a thunderous noise broke the silence and something big and heavy landed on the roof. Sarah jumped. Feeling trapped in her sleeping bag, she tried to squirm out of the cocooned bundle as quickly as she could. Maggie let out a soft squeal and began scampering out of her sleeping bag too. Rick, somehow, managed to jump right out of his bag, in one swift movement. The creature moved around above them. The roof dipped slightly as the creature moved. They stood close together, nobody made a sound, as they tried to figure out what it could be.

"I'm going out," whispered Rick, picking up his shoe that lay close by.

Rick jumped out of the shelter and shouted like a crazy, mad man. The creature squawked and flew off.

"It was just an owl," said Rick, shrugging his shoulders.

Both girls sighed in relief and then began giggling nervously.

"You looked so funny jumping out there, with just your shoe in your hand. What were you going to do with it?" laughed Maggie, through her words.

"I was going to throw it at that thing," Rick gestured towards the owl that was now long gone. Rick puffed out his chest like a strong brave man.

"Don't worry girls, I will protect you," he said mockingly.

"Huh," mumbled Maggie, "This should be interesting!"

"Well, I am not sleeping over there alone, now," said Sarah.

She dragged her sleeping bag as close to Maggie's, as she could get it.

"Are you sure you don't want to just get into mine with me?" Maggie joked, as she watched Sarah move even closer.

"Nope, this will do."

"Should we try this again," said Rick, climbing back into his sleeping bag.

"Yes," replied Maggie and slid into hers. She had to pull bits of it from underneath Sarah. She tugged and almost rolled Sarah right over. The girls started to laugh again. Maggie pulled her bag straight and climbed in. They all snuggled down and silence fell over them once again. Within minutes Sarah could hear Rick breathing deeply. She hated being the last to fall asleep. Closing her eyes, she tried to push all thoughts from her mind and relax. She breathed in deeply and then out, in and out.

"Sarah, wake up," whispered Maggie.

"What's going on?" asked Sarah, trying to focus on Maggie's face.

"Look," said Maggie, pointing at the ocean, through the open door.

"I have been awake for a while. I was watching the sunrise when I spotted them."

"Oh wow, there must be a hundred of them," whispered Sarah.
They starred at the school of dolphins swimming across the ocean, in front of them. The dolphins jumped in and through the waves. They seemed so close, Sarah felt as if she could just reach out and touch them.

"I have always wanted to swim with dolphins. Maybe I will get my chance sooner than I thought," said Sarah.
She could only imagine how awesome it would be to dive into the waves and swim with the beautiful, grey-blue creatures.

"Mmm, me too," Maggie simply said.
The girls were so mesmerised by the view that the sudden rumble of noise in the background nearly scarred the skin right off of them. Sarah and Maggie screamed at the same time. Rick bolted up in his sleeping bag.

"What?" he said, then heard the noise.
He shook off his sleeping bag and stood up, still trying to get his bearings.
Confused, he looked outside, then up at the sky.

"What is that?" asked Rick.
The noise stopped.

"You mean, what *was* that?" whispered Maggie.

"It sounded like a rumble," whispered Sarah back.

"I thought it was thunder," said Rick, looking out at the sky again. He was still half asleep.

"Whatever it was, it was loud and came from in there," said Maggie, pointing at the forest.

"Well, it's stopped now."

"What time is it?" asked Rick, rubbing his face with both hands.

"Almost six," said Maggie, looking at her wrist watch.

"Six? That is way too early. I am going back to sleep," moaned Rick.

"Oh no, you don't," said Maggie, pulling at his sleeping bag.

"We need to get exploring."

Rick groaned and stretched. He walked over to the fire place. The wood was still warm.

"I slept so well," he said, almost to himself.

"We just saw this huge school of dolphins swimming past. It was so amazing to see," Sarah told him, excitedly.

"How long have you two been up?"

"Not long," said Sarah. "But tomorrow I am getting up at the same time so I can go into the water with those dolphins."

Rick just looked at her like she was crazy, and then turned back to the fire. He had managed to re-ignite the wood already in the fireplace and added a few fresh pieces. Sarah just shrugged and busied herself with the breakfast, as her mind drifted back to the dolphins. Everyone got on with a chore, Maggie filled the kettle with water, Sarah got the pan and some eggs while Rick placed the tripod and grid on top of the fire. They had soon forgotten about the loud, thunderous noise, they had heard earlier.

Over breakfast they discussed their plan for the day. Rick was responsible for packing the 'survival' gear: torch; rope; compass; map and Swiss knife. Maggie planned to pack the food and water, while Sarah would check the other gear they needed: raincoats; jackets; sunblock and hats. Once breakfast was cleared away the friends began their chores for the trip. Each packed a small backpack. They closed up the shelter, checked the fire was completely out then headed down the longer stretch of beach, to the one side of their camp.

5
FOLLOW THE LEADER

"Okay, so we will follow the beach until we can find a clearing in the forest. Then we can head in and see what we find. Happy with that?" asked Rick, as he walked along the sand.

"Yip," replied the girls.

They all had good, firm walking boots on, with shorts and long sleeved tops so they would not get too scratched up by the bushes. The girls had wide brimmed hats while Rick had his trusty farmers hat on. They had sun-blocked from head to toe, before leaving and wore sunglasses to protect their eyes.

The tide was low and the waves rolled in gently from the ocean. It was early in the morning but the sun was already hot as it burned in the sky. As they walked on, Sarah looked back to see how far they were from camp. She could no longer see the shelter and the beach front they had left disappeared as they walked around an outcrop of rocks. A new stretch of beach lay in front of them. It wasn't as long as the beach they had landed on. In front of them was the start of a cliff, that seemed to hang suspended from the sky and loom over the water, then disappear beneath the swell. When they reached the cliff Rick looked into the thick bush.

"This is the end of the beach, girls. Looks like we are going to have to make our way through here or turn back?" he said, looking at the girls for a response.

"What if we get lost?" said Sarah, nervously.

"If we leave some markers along the way, we should be able to find our way back to the beach. I also have the compass, so we can use it to get back, to camp."

"Okay but what are we going to use as markers?" asked Maggie.
Rick thought for a moment.

"We need something that is visible and hardy," said Rick.

"What about marking the trees with grooves, using your knife?" asked Maggie.

"We could but if we come in from a different direction it may not be so easy to spot. Have you got any clothing we can cut up?" asked Rick.

"Not really. Wait, what about the dish towel? I wrapped the bread with one," said Maggie.

"Good idea," replied Rick.
Maggie removed her backpack, opened it and removed the bread. She unwrapped it and

handed the cloth to Rick. Sarah helped her to pack the bread away while Rick cut the cloth into thin strips.

Rick stepped into the bush and began pushing his way through the twigs and branches, being careful to hold them back so the girls could make their way through, behind him. After 20 steps he tied a piece of cloth to a branch and continued on. Rick did this every so often, making sure the pieces were not too close together but just enough to make sure they did not get lost. He checked the compass then changed direction slightly to ensure they were still on track.

"What about spiders and snakes?" Sarah suddenly asked, the thought creeped her out. She got a cold shiver down her spine and shook her body.

"Watch where you are going and what you are stepping on. You should be fine," Rick said casually.

"Right," said Sarah looking around and then down at the ground. She was terrified of both and did not feel like meeting either a snake or a spider.

"Actually, it would be cool to know what wildlife there is here. I wonder what animals survive on an island like this?" said Rick, with curiosity.

"I don't think I want to know," said Sarah, still looking around nervously.

"Me neither," said Maggie, starting to feel a bit unsure about this adventure.

"Come on, girls. This is all part of the fun. We are explorers, remember!" said Rick.

"Mmmhmm," Sarah replied, not sure she still agreed.

They walked for a while longer, in silence. Suddenly, Sarah yelled.

"Rick, here is one of our markers. Are we going in a circle?"

"Where?" said Rick, looking around.

Sarah pointed at a tree, not too far from where she was standing. Rick had walked right passed it. He dropped his head to hide his smile.

"You planned this? You sneaky rat!" wailed Maggie, punching her brother on the arm.

"I had to check that you were paying attention. I can't do all the work here. Oh, look I had the compass upside down. Silly me. Sorry girls, I will pay more attention."

Rick laughed.

"Grrr," growled Sarah.

"Boys!"

The girls both shook their heads and sighed.

"We are playing follow the leader, and our leader is lost," said Sarah.

"I am not lost," said Rick, defensively.

"Just testing you. Come on, this way."
Maggie looked around to check he was not messing around, again and then caught up to him. Sarah followed close behind.

A rustling noise above them, startled Sarah. She shot a glance up, to see monkeys swinging from tree to tree above her. There were a few mothers carrying babies on their tummies. Sarah smiled. She loved animals and nature.

The sun was glistening between the trees, directly above them as they came out at a large open field. Soft, long, green grass covered a massive flat piece of land in front of them. The grass field was met by a high mountain of black jaggered rocks on the one side. The surface of the mountain was completely black with not a single plant in sight. It was an unusual, but beautiful picture. The green grassed patch, with the black rocky back drop, enclosed in a circle of tall, thick trees looked like a painting, in a museum.

"Oh, wow. Is that a volcano?" asked Rick.

"I think so," said Maggie.

"There aren't many plants growing on the hillside. Do you think it's active?" asked Sarah.

"I don't think so," said Rick, looking around.

"Or none of this would be here."
He pointed at the grass and bush around them. They walked through the tall grass towards the other end of the forest. Rick was looking around suspiciously and stopped suddenly.

"Is that a pathway?" he said.
The girls stopped and looked in the same direction.

"I think it is," said Maggie.

"Yeah, there is a gap in the trees and no ground cover over there," Sarah pointed at the ground beneath the trees.

"How is that possible? Do you think there are people here?" asked Rick.
Sarah stepped closer to Maggie. The girls looked around as though they were being watched.

"Do you think there are other people here?" Sarah whispered to her friend.

"I don't know but that path looks well used."

"Let's have lunch here in the opening. It's just after midday and I am pretty hungry," said Rick, looking up at the position of the sun then removing his backpack and settling into the tall grass as it parted to form a gap for his body. The girls sat down with him, putting their bags down beside them. Maggie unpacked the food but kept glancing around. Sarah sat with her back to the mountain so she could see if there was any movement from the forest. Her eyes danced around the high branches and through the thicker bushes, wondering if someone was watching them. They chomped away at their sandwiches and then crunched through an apple each, all the while feeling like someone was watching them through the trees. After swallowing a gulp of water Rick stood up and looked at the path.

"Right let's go girls. We need to get ourselves back to the camp before sunset," he said.

The girls packed the leftover food away and stuck the water bottles into the sides of their backpacks. Following Rick, they headed back into the forest along the path they had found. The path continued a small distance from the edge of the forest and then came out at another open space. This time, there was a magnificent waterfall flowing from the mountain, into a rocky pool below. The mountain had changed from black rock to brown and green. Small plants and bushes grew along one side of the waterfall. At the top of the waterfall more trees and plants were scattered around.

"I am pretty sure that is a volcano," said Rick, pointing at the mountain to their left.

"And that is a normal mountain. Look at the plants on that one compared to that one." He pointed back to the mountain in front of them.

"Do you think we can drink this water?" asked Maggie.

"I would think so. Remember, if the water is flowing it is normally drinkable," said Rick.

"Yes, I remember reading about that," said Sarah.
Rick bent down and touched the water. It was cool and clear. He scooped a bit into his hand and sipped from it. The water tasted sweet and refreshing.

"Yip, that is fresh water," said Rick.
The girls bent down and did the same.

"Oh, wow. That is good," said Sarah.

"Let's fill our water bottles."

"Good idea. Then we need to mark the track so we know how to get back here. We will soon need more fresh water at the camp and it will help to know where we can find some," said Rick.

Everyone scratched through their bags to find their water bottles. Topped them up and drank from them, then refilled the bottles. After putting them away they turned to leave. Rick checked the compass and looked around to find the path.

"If we go back that way," he pointed at the path they had come from, "We will land up back at the volcano, so we need to find another path that leads in that direction."
He pointed to the right. They looked around.

"There," said Sarah, pointing at another opening in the trees, with yet another path.

"This is weird. There must be people here or maybe people used to be here," Rick said, shrugging his shoulders.
The girls looked around, feeling nervous again about being watched.

"I am getting creeped out," said Sarah.

"Let's go, please," said Maggie nervously.

"Yeah, I agree," said Sarah, sounding as nervous as she felt.
The three friends made their way, carefully into the forest, looking around for any sign of movement or sounds. Rick stepped onto a

branch, that made a loud crack and a flock of birds, in a nearby tree, squawked and flew off. Maggie and Sarah jumped. Rick started laughing.

"Will you just relax. It's just some birds," he said, through his laughter.

"It's not funny, Rick. I really feel like someone is watching us," moaned Maggie.

"Reveal yourselves," shouted Rick, with his hand raised like a warrior.
They stood quietly and listened. Nothing.

"See? Nobody here," said Rick, as he pushed on along the path.
At last, the path led out to the beach. Rick checked the compass again and pointed left.

"The camp should be that way,' he said and headed off in that direction.

"I feel so much better now that we are out of the forest," said Sarah.

"Me too," sighed Maggie, with relief.

"There's the camp," said Rick, pointing at their little shelter.

"Wow, that was awesome and we made it before sunset."
They all began to walk a little faster, happy to see their shelter, until they were only a few steps away.

"Ah, man, what..." groaned Rick, as he looked around the camp.

They stopped dead in their tracks. The shelter was open and the crates had been turned upside down. Food was lying all around and their water tank had been tipped over. Sarah began to cry.

"It's okay," said Maggie, putting her arm around her friend.

"Who could have done this? I told you someone was watching us," wailed Sarah, through her tears.

"I don't know,' said Rick, picking up their stuff and packed it back into the crates.

6
PEEK-A-BOO, I SEE YOU

That night, as they sat around their fire, Rick set out his plan.

"We need to get back out there again tomorrow and see if we can find anyone, but we will need to make sure we protect our stuff," said Rick, drawing with a stick in the sand.

"How are we going to do that?" asked Sarah.

"Set some traps," said Rick.

"What kind of traps?" asked Maggie, a little nervously.

"Well," Rick continued drawing in the sand.

"We need to try and capture our invaders," he said, like a pirate.

"We could build a catch into the shelter that would slam close when someone tries to open one of the crates. Then they would be locked inside. Plus, we could set a rope up in one of the trees, so when they stand on the loop – they will be snapped up and trapped."

"And you know how to do this, right?" said Maggie, sarcastically.

"Of course," said Rick, confidently.

"Okay, but what will we do with them, once we have them trapped?" asked Sarah.

"Bury them in the sand so only their heads stick out. Then we can get information out of them," said Rick with a laugh, sounding a little like a crazy person.

"You are really enjoying the idea of being an adventurer, aren't you?" said Maggie, giggling at Rick as he stood and swung his stick around like a sword.

"Boys live for this kind of adventure," he said, jumping around like he was having a sword fight.

They all laughed, forgetting for a moment that there was someone else out there.

"For now, we need to get some sleep. I am exhausted," said Rick through a yawn.

"I don't know if I can," said Sarah.

"Me neither," said Maggie.

"I don't think they mean to harm us. Maybe they were just nosey. If they have been here a while they may not have seen some of this stuff before," said Rick, pointing at all their equipment.

"Maybe, but how can we be sure?" said Maggie.

"Okay, I will make a latch to close the shelter so nobody can get in," said Rick.

He walked over to the shelter and looked around the inside of the door, trying to work out how he could keep it closed. The girls began packing their dinner plates away. Rick quickly got to work creating a latch for the door while the girls sat at the fire keeping warm. The night was cooler than the one before. Clouds had started to form in the dark sky, hiding most of the stars.

"What will we do if it rains tomorrow?" Maggie asked Rick.

"We need more water, so we will have to go back into the forest, to the waterfall. Raining or not," he said, sternly.

"Or we could just put containers out and catch the rain water," said Sarah.

"Good idea, Sarah," said Maggie.
Rick looked up and nodded in agreement.

"Yeah, good idea."
Sarah smiled, feeling proud of herself.

"Right, that should do it," said Rick, stepping back to admire his work.
The girls got up and walked over to see what he had done.

"That's pretty good, Rick," said Sarah.

"I feel safer already."

"You're such a clever boy," teased Maggie, ruffling her older brother's hair.

Rick ducked and tried to dodge Maggie's teasing.

"Get off it," he said, blushing.

"Ah, what's the matter Ricky?" Maggie continued to tease, as she chased her brother around trying to rub his head again.

"Stop or I'll…"

"You'll what?" said Maggie, still trying to get at his head.

"I'll break your fingers," he said, leaping forward and tackling his sister.

Maggie screamed as she fell to the ground. Rick jumped on top of her and began ruffling her hair until it was knotty.

"Stop, stop, please stop," Maggie yelled, through her laughter.

Sarah just stood laughing, as she watched the two of them playing around.

"You two…" she said and walked out of the shelter.

Rick climbed off his sister and helped her up. They started out the shelter, to follow Sarah when suddenly there was a scream. Rick dashed out ahead of Maggie, almost knocking her over.

"What?" he called out, as he came to stand next to a frozen Sarah.

"There," she pointed into the trees.
Rick could make out a figure with long arms and a round head, sitting in the trees.

"Come down here and show yourself," Rick yelled at the dark outline.
The figure did not move for a few seconds and then suddenly vanished into the trees.

"What was that?" asked Sarah.

"What? What can you see?" Maggie asked, running up behind them.

"There was someone in the trees over there but now they're gone," whispered Sarah.

"Or so we hope," said Rick.
They all stared on into the forest for a while, waiting to see if the figure came out again. After a long while Rick walked back to the fire. Sarah thought back about the monkeys she had seem in the forest.
Could it have been a monkey, she thought.

"So what are we going to do now?" asked Sarah, even more nervous than before.

"Nothing, we need to get some sleep. We will be safe inside. Let's just make sure we leave nothing outside," he said, getting up and walking around the camp site.

They all checked the site and then headed into the shelter. Rick stopped at the door.

"You girls get changed and then I will come in," he said, closing the door behind him and heading back to the fire.

The girls quickly changed into more comfortable sleeping clothes and then gave Rick a chance to use the shelter to change. They stood around the fire, with their backs to the ocean, watching the dark outline of trees in front of them.

It was quiet, too quiet, thought Sarah. Now that they knew there was someone out there, everything felt eerie and mysterious. Sarah didn't enjoy the not knowing. When Rick was done he killed the fire completely and locked the three of them inside the shelter. He double checked the lock, pulling hard on the door. It didn't budge. Satisfied, he climbed into his sleeping bag. The girls did the same, only they had moved their beds closer to Rick's and each other. They lay neatly in a row, like three little peas in a pod, listening for any sound. The odd sound of an owl tooted somewhere in the distance and the wind had started to blow a gentle whisper through the trees above them. Sarah shivered. She snuggled closer to Maggie.

Sarah lay awake for what felt like ages. Just as she thought she could fight sleep no more, the door on the shelter shook. All three friends let out a roaring scream. Rick jumped out of his sleeping back and ran towards the door. While he quickly removed the knotted lock a thump sounded on the roof and then another as the creature ran across the top of the shelter. By the time Rick had made it outside the intruder was gone.

"This is going to be a long night," said Rick wearily, as he came back into the shelter.
He locked the door once more and lay down.

"I'll stay awake and keep guard," said Rick.

"You girls try and get some sleep."

"Are you sure? What about you?" said Maggie with concern.

"I'll feel better when we catch this thing," said Rick, angrily.

"Get some sleep."
Maggie and Sarah lay down and tried to sleep.
Sarah woke to the sound of hard rain hitting the roof of the shelter. Rick and Maggie were fast asleep. She was glad to see that Rick had finally managed to fall asleep. Sarah lay quietly, listening to the rain fall. The shelter didn't seem to be leaking anywhere, which was a

good thing. It was still very dark outside but Sarah did not want to wake anyone by getting up to check the time. She closed her eyes and drifted off to sleep again.

When Sarah finally woke, the sun was streaming through the open door of the shelter. Sarah sat bolt upright. She quickly looked around, relieved to see that Rick and Maggie were no longer in their sleeping bags. She got up and headed outside. It was a beautiful morning. The ocean was rough and the waves rolled in close to their camp. There was no sign that the rain had pounded down the night before. The sky was clear and blue as it made its way above the horizon.

"Good morning, sleeping beauty?" said Rick.

"Good morning," replied Sarah, smiling, as she stretched and then sat down next to Maggie.

"How did you sleep?" asked Maggie.

"Good thanks. And you?" asked Sarah.

"Really good. Did I imagine it or was it raining last night?" asked Maggie.

"Yeah, it came down in buckets. Wouldn't say so looking around this morning," said Sarah, looking across the beach.

"How long have you been up?" asked Sarah.

"Not sure but we were woken by that loud noise again," said Maggie.

"Yeah, it seems to be the same time each morning. Weird," said Rick.

"Hmm. And any sign of our mystery intruder?" asked Sarah.

"Nope," said Rick, as he fiddled with the fire for breakfast.

"Are we still planning to set traps today?" Maggie asked.

"Yip, sure are. I am not letting that rascal near our stuff again. We are going to catch him once and for all," said Rick bravely.

"And we are still going to get water?" asked Sarah, trying to work out the plan for the day.

"That's right," said Rick, getting up and heading for the shelter.

"So what are we doing for breakfast?" asked Sarah.

Maggie raised the bowl in front of her.

"Eggs."

"What can I do?" responded Sarah.

"You could get the pan and spatula. Oh and a separate bowl so I can separate your eggs, Miss Fussy-pants!"

Sarah pulled her tongue out at Maggie, as she got up to collect the stuff Maggie had asked for. She sat down next to Maggie and picked up two eggs. She cracked them and separated the white from the yellow, placing them in separate bowls.

"There done. No fuss," said Sarah, nudging her friend.

"Thank you," replied Maggie.

While the girls finished preparing the breakfast, Rick began working on his traps. First he started with the door. He made sure that it closed on its own and swung into the latch he had made on the inside. Then he secured the catch on the outside so it would lock as soon as the door closed. He checked and re-checked.

"Um, can someone let me out, please," Rick called, from inside the shelter.

The girls started giggling. Maggie got up to let her brother out.

"Well, at least you know it works," said Maggie, as she freed Rick from his own trap.

"Yip, but I don't want to be testing the other trap quite the same way," said Rick, pointing up at the trees.

When the girls realised what he meant, they started laughing.

"No, you sure don't because we might just leave you hanging there," laughed Maggie.

After breakfast, the girls cleared away while Rick went to work on his second trap. He made sure that nothing was lying around the area and warned the girls to stay clear. He climbed the tree and threw the rope over a firm, thick branch. Once the rope was hanging down to the ground, on both sides, he climbed down and tied it tightly to the large rock he had balancing on a larger bolder. He then set a trip rope that would force the rock to roll forward once the rope was touched. The loop on the opposite side would then tighten and trap the person's foot, hoisting them high into the air. The person would then be left dangling until they found him. Rick stepped back and admired his work. He double checked everything was in place before returning to the girls.

Rick was happy to see that the girls were ready. They had packed containers, to fill with water and one small backpack with just the basics. Rick made sure the fire was out and the door to the shelter was not closed properly. He wanted to be sure to trap the intruder. He then checked his compass and set off down the beach in the direction they had come from the day before. Once they found the path, the markers they had set out were not necessary. The path led straight to the waterfall. Before they could get a few feet into the forest, they heard a weird shriek and loud screams coming from the shelter. Rick began running as fast as he could. The girls followed at a slower pace. Rick reached the beach as the screams grew louder. When he was only a short distance from the camp the noises stopped. He continued running until he reached the camp. The shelter door now stood wide open. Rick did not slow down as he ran past the door and on towards his second trap. The rope had been cut and the smaller boulder now lay on the beach. He took off his hat and threw it on the ground in frustration. The intruder had gotten away.

As Rick stood staring in disbelief at his failed trap, the girls came running up behind him. They were both out of breath.

"What happened?" asked Sarah.

"He got away," growled Rick.

"He? I think there was more than just one, Rick," said Maggie.

"One person could not get caught and escape both traps in such a short time. Plus, it sounded like more than one person screaming," she added, matter-of-factly. Rick scratched his head then turned and walked back to the shelter. He stood staring at the door.

"I think you are right, Maggie. Only I think there are more than two or three of them," said Rick.

"Oh, boy. What have we gotten ourselves into," wailed Sarah.

"Relax," said Rick.

"The way they were crying and screaming, I don't imagine they are giants."

"Right, well that's good to know," said Maggie, not trusting her own words.

"So, what now? We have to find out who is causing so much trouble," said Sarah.

"We could head back into the forest and try to find them," said Rick.

"No way. We have no idea who they are," said Sarah.

"Maybe we should turn the game around. If we stalk them without them knowing then maybe we can find out what's going on," said Maggie.

"And how do we do that?" asked Rick.

"I don't know. You're the boy here. Surely you can come up with a plan," said Maggie, looking at Rick with wide eyes.

"Okay, let me think," Rick said and sighed.

"I'll get lunch ready," said Sarah, keen to keep busy.

"I'll tidy up the mess," said Maggie and walked off towards the shelter.

Rick paced up and down, deep in thought.

"I've got it," he finally said with excitement. Both girls turned to look at him, waiting to hear his plan.

"We will pretend we are packing up and head down the beach again. But this time we will hide in the trees just a short way away from the camp so we can see who appears," Rick whispered loudly.

"Yes, that's a great idea," said Sarah, just as excited.

Maggie nodded eagerly.

The team picked up their bags and started heading off down the beach once more. After a short distance they ducked into the trees and crouched down. Quietly, they waited. And waited. And waited. It felt like they had been sitting there for hours until Rick finally spoke.

"I think the traps have scared them away," he said.

"We still need water," commented Maggie.

"Okay, let's go," said Rick.

"What about the camp?" asked Sarah.

"We've closed everything up. It doesn't look like they will be back for a while to bother us," Rick said, shrugging his shoulders.

"We have no choice."

The three friends crept out of the bush, staying close to the trees they made their way back to the path that led to the waterfall. The walk was not long and before they knew it, they were standing in front of the waterfall. Quickly, the girls began to fill their containers. They placed the smaller ones in their bags and picked up the bigger ones to carry. Maggie stood up and looked around.

"Ow, what was that for?" cried Rick, as Maggie slapped his arm, hard.

Rick first looked up at his sister and then followed her eyes to the top of the waterfall. There stood two boys. They looked about ten years old. As soon as they realised Rick and Maggie had spotted them, they disappeared behind the rocks. Sarah stood up and looked up too.

"What are you looking at?" asked Sarah, unaware of what they had just seen.

"Back up quickly and quietly. Let's get out of here," was all Rick said.
Nervously, Sarah grabbed her containers and started towards the path. Maggie and Rick followed quickly behind her. Sarah kept turning around to check they were still there. Rick kept glancing back to make sure nobody was following them. They reached the camp and Rick nudged them all inside, locking the door behind them.

"What is going on?" asked Sarah, totally confused.

"There were two boys watching us from the top of the waterfall," Maggie blurted out.
Sarah sat down on the sand and Maggie sat down beside her. The girls looked terrified.

"It's going to be okay," said Rick. "They looked as frightened as we are."

"Well I am tired of playing hide and seek, This is getting really freaky," said Maggie.

7
"WHERE'S MY HAT?"

For the rest of the day, the three friends stayed at camp. Nobody really said much as they all thought about the boys they had seen. As the sun began to set, Maggie kept busy by preparing dinner. Sarah helped while Rick prepared another fire, to cook their meal.

"I think we should go back tomorrow and try to talk to them?" said Rick, breaking the silence.

"What if they are mean and try to harm us?" said Sarah.

"We won't know unless we try. Isn't that why we are here?" asked Rick.

"Yes, I suppose you're right," said Sarah, shrugging her shoulders.

"Okay, then let's get some sleep tonight and we can go up there tomorrow," said Rick.
That night everything was quiet. Waves rolled gently onto the shore and the moon hung bright and boldly in the sky. The three friends were so tired that they fell into their sleeping bags with exhaustion. Each one lay there wondering if someone was going to bang on their shelter again that night. But as the night grew darker there was no sound of people lurking outside. Eventually they fell asleep.

The next morning the sound of birds chirping and the rushing waves from the ocean woke Sarah. She quietly, got up and let herself out of the shelter. It was another beautiful day. In the distance she could see the sun just coming up on the horizon. Then she spotted them: The school of dolphins swimming even closer to the shore than before. Quickly, she ran back into the shelter, grabbed her swim suit and changed behind the sheet that hung in the shelter. Nobody moved as she slipped out and ran down to the beach. Sarah waded into the water. It was cool at first. She dived into an oncoming wave and began to swim out towards the dolphins. Just then she heard someone call her name. She stopped in the water and turned towards the shore. Maggie was waving.

"What are you doing?" called Maggie.

"Going to swim with the dolphins," shouted Sarah, pointing out to sea.

"Wait for me," replied Maggie, dashing back into the shelter.

Sarah continued to swim out slowly, stopping every now and then to check where Maggie was. Finally, Maggie caught up to her and they swam out towards the dolphins together.

When they were only a few meters away the dolphins began to head towards them, swimming underneath them and bumping them with their bodies. Sarah and Maggie squealed with excitement as they tried to touch the sneaky mammals. Eventually the dolphins slowed down and moved in closer, bobbing on the surface close to their faces. Sarah put out her hand and tried to touch one on the nose. The dolphin ducked away but quickly reappeared. Sarah kept her hand out. The dolphin continued to play with her until; at last, he let Sarah stroke his nose. Maggie had also made a new friend. The girls swam around while the dolphins moved between them, bumping and rubbing up against them. Sarah was so happy. It was a dream, come true.

After a long while the dolphins started to swim away. When they had all left, Sarah and Maggie made their way back to shore. Rick was standing on the beach watching them.

"Awesome," he shouted, as they pushed through the small waves towards him.

"Did you see them? It was amazing," said Sarah, dancing around the beach, with excitement.

Rick nodded his response as Maggie ran into the shelter to fetch two towels.

"That was pretty amazing!" said Maggie, to her brother when she came out.

"I bet. You should have woken me," said Rick, smiling at his sister's excitement.

"Sorry, Sarah was already heading out when I got up and I needed to catch up to her," said Maggie, feeling bad.

"That's okay. We have another adventure waiting for us today, remember?" said Rick.

"Oh, yes. I had almost forgotten," said Maggie, handing Sarah a towel.

"Umm, so did I," said Sarah, suddenly very serious.

"No time to waste. Let's get our stuff together and head back into the forest," said Rick, calmly.
Sarah and Maggie exchanged worried glances and then went off to pack their bags.

"Where's my hat?" Rick shouted from inside the shelter.

"I don't know," said Maggie. "You had it on yesterday. Where did you put it?"

"I was sure I put it on my bag," said Rick, scratching his head.

"I'll check inside again."

They joined Rick back on the beach. Rick still had no hat on.

"I can't find it," Rick moaned. "Let's just go."

Rick picked up his bag, in a huff and they made their way to the path that headed into the forest.

"How are we going to find them?" asked Sarah.

"We'll go back to the waterfall and see if they are there. If not then we will have to climb the hill to where we last saw them," explained Rick.

The girls said nothing, as they followed Rick along the now familiar path. Once they reached the waterfall they all began looking around suspiciously. Then suddenly Rick spotted movement on the rocks above.

"There," he said, excitedly and started waving at the boys.

The boys quickly ducked down. They waited, watching the spot where they had seen them appear. Slowly, two heads reappeared behind the rocks.

"Hello," shouted Rick.

He waved his hands like a crazy person. The boys looked at each other. The bigger of the two boys, slowly, raised his hand and waved back.

"See, they are friendly," said Rick, turning to the girls.

Sarah was now waving too. So Maggie raised her hand and gave a little wave. Everyone just stood there for a long while. Nobody dared to make the first move. Then as suddenly as the boys had appeared, they were gone. The friends stood at the bottom of the waterfall waiting. After a long while Rick picked up his bag.

"I'm going to head up there," he said.

"Are you sure?" said Maggie.

"Yip, they seem harmless," said Rick.

Just as Rick was about to head off there was a thump behind him. He turned to see his hat lying on the ground with a large stone inside.

"Sneaky rats. They took my hat," said Rick, through gritted teeth.

"Oooo, I'll..." his voice trailed off.

He bent down and picked up his hat. Dusting it off, he put it on his head. Pulling it firmly over his ears, he turned and marched off towards the path.

"I thought we were going to go and meet them?" asked Maggie, pointing towards the hill, a little confused.

"Not after they turned out to be thieves," said Rick, angrily.

Once again the girls just followed Rick back to the beach.

When they reached the shelter they found an empty, woven basket lying at the fireplace. The basket was carefully crafted and looked as though food had been stored in it, from the pink stains that lined the inside.

"What's this?" said Sarah, picking up the basket.

"A peace offering maybe?" said Maggie, moving closer to take a look.

Rick just huffed and took the basket from Sarah. He studied it carefully.

"It's definitely manmade," he said, shrugging his shoulders and dropping it on the ground.

"Why would they leave it here?" said Sarah, confused by the gift.

"To let us know they have been here," said Rick, still in a huff.

"So if there were two of them on the hill that means that they could not have left it here. Which means..." Sarah trailed off.

"There are more of them," finished Maggie.

"Yip," said Rick, picking up the basket again.

"But why leave the basket?" said Maggie, trying to figure out the meaning.

"Who knows but I am tired of playing these games," said Rick and stormed off into the shelter, taking the basket with him.

"What do you think we should do?" asked Sarah.

"I'm not sure but we need to figure this out," said Maggie, going to sit on the sand.
Sarah sat down beside her and they stared out over the blue water. The sun blazed down and water crept slowly towards them, just tickling the tips of their toes.

"It's just a bit weird though. Why would they take Rick's hat and then leave a basket? Maybe they are trying to make contact but don't know how?" said Sarah, more to herself.

"Yes, you mean like sending a signal. Maybe they are trying to figure us out too," said Maggie, puzzled.

"I think we should go back again and try to talk to them," said Sarah.

Me too. I am a little nosey now to find out who they are. Aren't you?" said Maggie, with a slight grin on her face.

"Yeah, I am," said Sarah, smiling back at her friend.

They both giggled.

"I wonder where they came from. Or do you think they were born here?" continued Sarah.

"I don't know. How many do you think there are?" asked Maggie.

Sarah shrugged her shoulders as her mind drifted off.

"Umm, I wonder," said Maggie, lost in her own thoughts.

"What are you girls talking about?" asked Rick, sitting down next to Maggie.

"Just wondering about those boys," said Maggie.

"Well, I think we should find out where they are hiding so I can give them a piece of my mind," said Rick, getting all worked up again.

"Oh, stop. You're being a grouch. You were the one who said they were the reason we are here. So let's just try to get to know them and we can figure it out from there," said Maggie to her brother.

"Mmmm. Okay. What's the plan?" he asked.

"I think we should get to the top of the hill so we can find them," said Sarah, suddenly feeling excited about the adventure.

"Yeah, I want to know more about them," said Maggie.

"Me too," Rick admitted.

"Right, so tomorrow we are going up the hill?" said Maggie, looking from Rick to Sarah.

"Yes," they answered together.

8
MYSTERY SOLVED

"Wakey, wakey," whispered Rick, as he shook the girls gently.

"Time to rise and shine. Time to go exploring."
Both girls moaned. Sarah rolled over and glanced out the door. The sky was grey and the water was dull and murky.

"What time is it?" asked Maggie, rubbing her eyes and stretching.

"Time to rock and roll," said Rick, walking out to the camp fire.
Maggie climbed out of her sleeping bag, walked over to a stump near the fire and sat down. Sarah grabbed her jacket, pulled it around her shoulders and sat down next to Maggie.

"Looks like it might rain," she said.

"Mmm," responded Maggie, still half asleep.

"I could have slept all day."

"Not today. Today we are going to sort this problem," Rick waved his hand from side to side, towards the trees.

"Once and for all."
Once they were all dressed and breakfast was cleared away, they prepared their bags, to head into the forest, once again. Maggie was

tossing stuff about the shelter in search of her water bottle.

"Um, guys, my water bottle is missing," she said.

"That does it," said Rick, picking up his bag.

"Let's go, you can share my water."

Once they reached the waterfall, Rick headed left, towards the hillside. The hill rose steeply above them but Rick could make out a distinct path leading up and around the climb. He walked on ahead of the girls, being sure to keep an eye on the path ahead. The girls followed, watching their footing for loose stones and branches. Rick stopped suddenly. He put out his hand behind him to stop Maggie from walking straight into the back of him. Maggie stopped and Sarah almost bumped straight into the back of her.

"Why...," she started.

"Shhh," whispered Rick.

"I heard something."

Sarah held her breath and stood dead still. They all listened. Suddenly, birds screeched and escaped from the tree above them, scaring the daylights out of all three of them. They jumped in fright but did not move a step. Once the birds had vanished and all was quiet again,

Rick listened. Nothing. He waited a little while longer and then kept walking. He signaled for the girls to walk on quietly, behind him. They tiptoed, almost holding their breath as they crept slowly towards the top of the hill. Out of nowhere, a boy stepped into their path, with his arms crossed and a very serious look on his face. The three friends gasped and caught their breath, coming to an immediate halt in front of the boy.

"What you want?" asked the boy.

"Um, we, um, came to meet you?" said Rick nervously.

"Why you here?" said the boy.

"We," Rick pointed towards the girls, "Are explorers."
The boy looked confused.

"What your name?"

"I am Rick, this is Maggie and Sarah," he pointed at each person as he introduced them.

"What is your name?" Asked Maggie, gently as she peeked from behind Rick.
The boy looked past Rick and directly at Maggie.

"Tim," was all he said.

"Nice to meet you Tim."
Maggie extended her hand.

The boy looked at her hand and then hit it. He smiled and put out his hand for Rick to hit. Rick hit his hand. Then Tim extended his hand to Sarah. Sarah smacked his hand with hers, trying not to giggle.

"Come," said Tim, turning and walking up the hill.

Rick turned to look at the girls, shrugged his shoulders and followed Tim. The girls exchanged glances and then followed Rick.

When they reached the top of the hill, a stream of water was gushing from the flat top of the hill as it rushed towards the end and fell into the pool below. Rick peaked over and could see the spot they had once stood, below. When Rick looked up the boy was skipping from rock to rock, like someone who had crossed the river often, until he reached the other side. There he stopped to check on his visitors. Rick looked carefully from rock to rock and began to move more slowly across the stream. Maggie and Sarah stayed close behind, following Rick's every move. When all three had reached the other side, the boy turned and continued to follow the stream. They walked for some time before Rick realised that the sandy hill had become black stone beneath their feet.

"Where are we going?" asked Rick.

"To cave," said the boy, pointing at the volcano that now loomed above them.

"Cave? Is that where you live or are you tricking us?" asked Rick, suspiciously.

"What this tricking mean?" asked the boy. Rick thought for a second and then said, "What is in the cave?"

"My brothers," said Tim.

"Ah, right. So, you live in the cave?" asked Maggie.

"Yes," said Tim, simply.

"Cool," said Maggie.

Tim looked confused by Maggie's comment but turned and kept walking. Rick turned to the girls and signaled with his thumbs up to be sure the girls were happy to go on. Both girls gave the 'thumbs up' sign and so Rick continued to follow Tim.

They finally reached a small break in the large rock wall and Tim ducked inside. The three friends followed. The entrance only shed a little light on the tunnel ahead and it took some time for their eyes to adjust to the darkness. They could barely see down the long, tunnel-like passage winding on ahead of them.

"Come,' said Tim. "Brothers, there," he said, pointing at the unknown in front of them.

Finally they reached the end of the long passage and came out in a large, circular opening. The three friends looked up to see the sky, rising high above them. This opening gave the only light to the dark cave. In the centre was a massive fireplace, with large rocks surrounding the area. Tim let out a high screeching whistle that made the three friends cover their ears. One by one boys and girls began to creep out from behind the rocks. Sarah counted 14 children in total. None of them looked older than 12 years old. The youngest, a little girl looked just 4 or 5 years old. She hid behind an older girl that looked like her sister.

"Hello," said Sarah as she moved to stand next to Maggie.

"My name is Sarah, this is Maggie and Rick." The little girl peeped her head around at the sound of Sarah's voice. Sarah smiled at her. The little girl ducked behind her sister again. Tim moved forward and waved his hands for the children to move closer.

"We not all have name. Only the one who remember. This Ben; Franklin; Peter; Hendry and Cliff. This Mary; Sof; Chalet," introduced Tim, as he pointed at the bigger children in the group.

"We say Baby; Boy and Thumb for this one," he said pointing at the three smallest children.

Rick; Maggie and Sarah smiled at the dirty faces starring back at them.

"Could Hendry be Henry?" asked Sarah.

Ah, yes. That right," said Henry.

"And Sof: Sophia."

Sophia nodded.

"Charlotte maybe?" asked Sarah.

"Yes, me Charlotte," replied the girl.

"They're all beautiful names," said Maggie. The girls beamed, proudly.

"Where are you from?" asked Rick.

Where do you think the children came from?

Use the lines on the next page to fill in this part of the book with your own idea of what you think happened to the children and how they ended up on the island.

Remember, you can send your story to me and stand a chance to win

Book #3 FREE.

Ask an adult to help you scan your page in and send it to me. My details are available on my website.

www.selfpublishersemporium.com

Author: Lara Hunter

Get creative... and enjoy!

I look forward to reading your story.

9
IT ALL MAKES SENSE NOW

"Wow," said Sarah. Amazed by the children's story.

"How have you managed to survive here, for so long?" asked Maggie.

"We must. It be easy after long time," said Peter, speaking up for the first time.

"Where do you sleep?" asked Sarah.

"In those holes," said Peter, pointing at the deep holes in the walls of the volcano.

"Doesn't it get dark in here during the night?" asked Maggie.

"No. Moon come in there," said Tim.

"This is a great fireplace," said Rick, admiring their large stones in and around the fire.

"We get from up there," responded Ben.
They all looked up at the opening above them. Sarah looked at Maggie, confused.

"Rocks get hot from sun. Burn light all night," explained Tim.
The three friends still looked confused.

"Come, I show you."
Tim let out three whistles and the other five boys ran off. They returned with large woven baskets on their backs. Tim picked up a woven sack, filled with water and headed towards the entrance of the cave.

"You come?" he said to Rick.

Rick quickly ran to catch up, then looked back at the girls.

"We'll be fine. You go," said Maggie.

Rick gave a short wave and continued to follow the group of boys.

Maggie and Sarah turned back towards the rest of the group. All the remaining children's eyes were now set on Maggie and Sarah. Neither of the girls knew what to say next. Then, Baby, the smallest girl came over and took Sarah's hand. Sarah knelt down next to the little girl. Baby raised her hand slowly and touched Sarah's hair.

"Soft," said Baby.

"Thank you," said Sarah, smiling at the little girl.

Baby touched her hair tie.

"I have some more back at our camp if you would like one?" asked Sarah.

Baby shook her head eagerly.

"Where you from?" asked Mary.

"We live in New Zealand," answered Maggie.

"We found this island on our map and decided to come and see what was here. We had no idea there were children living here," she continued.

"New Zelad. Where this place?" asked Sophia.

Maggie was not sure how to answer as she realized the children may not understand.

"Um, it is very far away. We came here by boat," she said.

"You got boat?" asked Mary, her eyes lit up. Mary seemed to be the oldest of the girls. Sophia and Charlotte looked a few years younger than Mary.

"Yes, we do. How old are you all?" asked Maggie, pointing at each of them.

"Me, 11, Sophia and Charlotte 9, Baby 4, Boy 4 and Thumb 5, he still smaller," said Mary, using her hand to show that Thumb was shorter than the younger children. The other children laughed. Thumb huffed and turned away.

"It's okay, Thumb. You will grow up too," said Maggie, touching him on the shoulder.
She felt bad for him. The other children obviously teased him because he was so short for his age. Thumb turned and smiled at Maggie and then took her hand. Maggie smiled back and squeezed his hand. He let go

suddenly and ran into a hole in the cave wall. When he returned he was holding Maggie's water bottle.

"Where did you find that?" asked Maggie.

"Monkey," said Thumb.

"Monkey?" said Maggie, confused.

"Bad monkeys. Bring from you cave to here," said Thumb.

"So it's the monkeys that keep taking our stuff from our camp?" asked Sarah.
Thumb seemed to not understand completely but nodded his head, yes.

"Did the monkey's take your basket and leave it in our camp?" asked Sarah.
Thumb nodded again.

"Well, that makes sense," said Maggie.

"Monkey very bad. They take all fings from us," said Thumb, scrunching his face to look angry.

"Right," said Maggie, through a giggle.

"Where do the monkey's live, Thumb?" asked Sarah.

"Twees," blurted Baby, before Thumb could answer.

"In the trees?" asked Maggie, to be sure she had the story right.

All three of the little children nodded their heads wildly.

"An day teal da food," said Boy for the first time, "den eat it up."
He pretended to gobble food from his hands. Maggie and Sarah began to laugh. The other bigger girls joined in. Boy looked around and then smiled and gobbled more imaginary food from his hands. The girls laughed louder. Boy loved the attention and began dancing around like a monkey, making noises and scratching under his arms. Everyone was laughing now.

"Come sit," said Mary, when the laughter had stopped.
The girls sat down, around the fire place and lifted some unfinished woven baskets, from the floor, beside them. They showed Maggie and Sarah how to weave the baskets and soon the girls were making a basket each. They chatted away about the island. Maggie and Sarah told them about their homes back in New Zealand. The children all listened with interest and asked them many questions.
Suddenly there was a loud whistle from the opening in the volcano. Mary and Sophia jumped up and ran to two long weaved ropes hanging from the opening. They tied a basket

to the one rope and began pulling on the other. Slowly the basket lifted up. It travelled all the way to the top. After a few moments, there was another whistle and the girls stopped pulling on the rope. Then two more whistles and the girls slowly pulled on the rope, then gently let it out. While the one rope loosened the basket slowly drifted back to the ground. It was full of large stones. Charlotte, Thumb and Boy had also got up and now stood near the basket with big palm leaves. They took each stone out carefully and placed it in the fireplace. Once the basket was empty, Mary began to pull on the rope again and the basket returned to the top of the volcano. A second basket was sent down filled with more stones and the children repeated their task. Three whistles sounded and the girls untied the basket and came to sit down at the fire place again.

"What are the stones for?" asked Sarah.

"Hot, hot," said Boy, as he pretended to touch them and shook his hand like he had been burnt. Maggie giggled.

"Make fire hot all night," said Mary, with a smile as she watched Boy showing off.

"We go now," said Sophia to the girls.

"Oh, where are we going?" asked Maggie.

"Get food," said Mary.

"Okay," said the girls together, getting up to follow.

"Basket," said Baby, pointing to the basket they had weaved.

Sarah and Maggie turned and went back to pick up their baskets. All the children headed out of the cave, each armed with a basket. The smaller children had baskets that were more the size of a bowl. They headed into the forest. Baby and Boy began picking berries from the small bushes and the older girls headed for some coconut trees. When they reached the base of the tree, Thumb began to climb the tree, just like a monkey. When he reached the top he removed a stone from his pocket and knocked away at the coconut. It loosened and then fell to the ground. Mary bent down and picked it up. She placed it in one of the baskets and waited for the next coconut then did the same again. Thumb climbed down and helped the girls to move the basket to the clearing near their cave. Next they headed down a separate path. This time they went a little deeper into the forest. Mary stopped at a thick bush and pulled it apart. Behind the bush was a trap. A dead rabbit was caught in the trap. Sarah suddenly felt sick and turned away. She did not enjoy seeing animals hurt or dead. Maggie touched her on the arm.

"Are you okay?" she asked.

"Yeah. I know it's for their food but it still makes me sad," said Sarah.

Mary passed the rabbit to Thumb. He lifted it up and had a good look at it.

"Food," he said, waving it at the girls.

Sarah gave a small smile then turned and walked away. Thumb seemed confused by Sarah's actions.

"You like babbit?" he asked, following Sarah.

"Um, sure," said Sarah, trying not to look at the dead creature.

Thumb placed the rabbit in the basket and walked on. A bit further down the track Mary found another trap. This time there were two large birds caught inside. She removed them and placed them in another basket.

Turning she headed back up the track towards the cave.

"We done," said Sophia, to the girls.

Maggie and Sarah followed, carrying their baskets with the dead animals inside. Sarah thought she might cry and kept her eyes straight ahead so she would not have to look inside her basket.

When they returned to the cave, the boys had arrived back. A giant fire burned brightly in the centre of the fireplace. Both girls watched with amazement.

"Wow, that is some fire," said Maggie.

"Yeah, and it's hot. I can feel it from here," said Sarah, standing a distance from the fire.

The older girls disappeared around a corner of the cave while the small children and the boys began to prepare the fruit and berries for their meal. Rick, Maggie and Sarah helped the boys while Rick told them about his trip up the volcano with the other boys. The girls listened with interest and then told Rick about the naughty monkeys.

"Well that all makes sense now. So the monkey's steal our stuff and put it in their camp and then do the same to them?" asked Rick as he pointed towards the other kids.

"Yip. Naughty rascals," said Sarah.

"Sure are," said Rick, in agreement.

"But knowing that, we probably should head back to our shelter. We have been gone

all day. Who knows what mischief those creatures have been up to."
The girls nodded in agreement. Rick walked over to Tim and explained that they had to leave. Sarah could see Tim nodding his head and the boys exchanging words. Then Rick returned to stand next to them.

"What did he say?" asked Maggie.

"He was hoping we would stay for dinner. I told him we would make a plan for tomorrow night when we are better prepared. Come on, let's say our goodbyes and head out before it gets too dark," said Rick, walking over to the children around the fire.

Rick lifted his hand and Tim slapped it. Keeping his hand in the air, Rick walked from child to child slapping hands with each of them. The girls came out from where they had been preparing the food and slapped hands with Rick. Thumb hugged Maggie around the legs. She rubbed his back and bent down to give Baby and Boy a hug. Sarah also hugged the three little children. They waved and headed out of the cave.

The walk back to the camp seemed quick and easy as they now knew their way around. As they got closer to the camp Rick began to run.

"What's wrong?" called Maggie, starting to run after him.

Sarah began running too, not sure what was going on.

"The camp, it's been ransacked," shouted Rick.

"Oh, no," said Maggie and Sarah as they all stopped in front of their camp.

Their belongings were scattered everywhere. The shelter had been ripped open and their clothes and bedding lay all over. The crates had been tipped upside down. The place was a mess.

"We can't sleep here tonight," said Rick angrily.

"The shelter doesn't look stable."

"So what are we going to do?" said Sarah, feeling helpless.

"We will have to gather our stuff together and go back to the children in the cave. We will be safer there," said Rick.

"Can you girls start packing up and I'll go back and get some help?" asked Rick.

"Sure," said Maggie.

"Yes, of course," agreed Sarah.

It was already getting dark and the girls struggled to see as they tried to gather everything together.

"Do you think Rick will be okay? It's getting darker and he might get lost," said Sarah, concerned.

"Yeah, he's been gone a long time. But I don't know what to do," said Maggie, worried.

"Let's get everything together and give him a little more time. Rick is smart. He will be fine," said Sarah, touching her friends arm.
Maggie nodded and continued to put their stuff into the crates. Sarah rolled up the bedding and packed clothes into bags.

"We're back," said Rick, out of the darkness.
Sarah and Maggie jumped in fright.

"You scared us," said Maggie.

"I am so glad you are okay though. You took forever."

"Yeah, it's a lot different walking through there in the dark," said Rick, pointing at the forest.
Tim, Ben and Cliff began picking up crates and headed back into the forest. Hendry and Franklin picked up a few bags and the bedding and followed the others. Maggie and Sarah

took the last few remaining things while Rick checked around the beach for any other items. When he was satisfied that they had everything he picked up the last crate and followed the group.

The walk through the forest was scary. The trees formed shadows and strange shapes around them. Eerie noises sounded above. Sarah shivered, feeling like things were crawling on her.

"I don't like this," said Sarah nervously.

"Just stick with the group and you will be fine," whispered Maggie.

"Why are you whispering?" whispered Rick, back.

"I don't know," whispered Maggie.
Sarah giggled. Maggie started giggling.

"And now, why are you giggling?" asked Rick, confused.

"We're nervous, okay," said Maggie, to her brother.

"Girls are so strange," said Rick, shaking his head.
The girls began giggling again. Suddenly, the boys ahead stopped dead and Sarah walked right into the back of Cliff. She moaned and then caught her breathe.

"What is it?" she asked, quietly.

"Stop. Box heavy," said Cliff.

"Oh," said Sarah, relieved it was nothing serious but started giggling again.

Maggie joined her.

"Why you laugh?" asked Tim.

"They are being silly," said Rick.

"What mean silly?" asked Tim.

Rick made a funny face and turned his finger around at the temple of his head pretending to be a crazy person. Tim started laughing. Rick pulled his face all funny and everyone started laughing at him.

"You like Boy and Thumb," said Tim, through his laughter.

This made everyone laugh even more. Still laughing the boys collecting up the crates and began walking again. Everyone followed. Soon they reached the cave. The girls came running towards them, helping the boys with the crates and smiling at the girls.

"Now you eat rabbit," said Sophia.

"Um, yes, rabbit," said Sarah, smiling politely.

Sarah was relieved to see the rabbit and other food already cooking on the fire. She was not sure she would have been able to eat the food, if she had watched the way in which they had prepared it. Now it just looked like roast chicken that her mum would make. Her tummy grumbled at the thought of food but she first helped to store away all their stuff, before joining the rest of the girls, around the fire.

Maggie sat down beside her with their plates and a fork each. Baby came over to Sarah and touched her fork. Sarah passed it to the little girl. She took it and turned it around, then pressed it to her cheek. She tried to bend it but it did not change shape. She stared at it in amazement.

"That's a fork," said Sarah, taking it from Baby and showing her how to eat with it.

The little girl watched as Sarah pretended to pick food up off her plate, with the fork and then put it to her mouth. She pretended to chew and then repeated the action. Baby's face beamed in amazement. She took the fork from Sarah and picked up some air off Sarah's plate and placed it in her mouth. She chewed on the imaginary food and then did it again. Thumb and Boy giggled as they watch Baby eating her imaginary meal. Maggie got up and walked over to one of their crates. She dug inside and removed another three forks, six dessert spoons and three teaspoons. She handed one to each child. They all looked at their new instruments with interest. Maggie returned to the crate and removed the large, sharp knife. She handed it to Rick. He got up and using his fork to hold the meat steady, cut into the rabbit. Everyone watched in stunned silence. They had never seen their meat being cut before. Rick took the piece of meat on his fork and passed it over to Tim. Tim removed the meat and placed it in his mouth.

"Ummm, good," he said.

"Me, Me, Me," the little children said, all at once.

Rick continued to cut pieces of meat off and pass them around to everyone. Sarah and Maggie just smiled at their innocence.

Everyone sat enjoying the meat that Rick passed out, until the rabbit was just a skeleton of bones. Mary got up to fetch a basket. She sat down, removed a piece of fruit and then passed the basket around. Each child took one fruit and passed it on. They sat in silence enjoying the juicy parcels in front of them. Once everyone was done Tim took a large leaf and began slapping the fire. The flames slowly died, sending smoke, high up into the funnel of the volcano. However, the rocks beneath glowed red with heat. Sarah was amazed at the heat she could feel coming from the rocks.

10
SMART KIDS

Sarah woke with a fright, as the loud thunderous noise sounded through the cave, closer than ever. She jumped up and ran into the centre of the cave. Rick was walking in from the entrance.

"Did you hear that noise again? It sounded so close," said Sarah.

"Yeah, it's the large boulder they roll in front of the entrance to keep animals out at night," said Rick.

"Right. Well that finally makes sense," said Sarah, relieved.

She turned and looked around her, as the children moved about. The cave was still as warm as it had been when they had gone to bed. She now understood what Rick had explained about the volcanic rock that the children used to keep the cave warm at night. It was amazing and she was very impressed with how they had figured it out. Tim was lighting the fire for breakfast while Mary was grinding seeds into powder. Maggie was sitting next to her chatting. Sarah walked over and sat down with them.

"Good morning. What are you making?" asked Sarah.

"Bread," replied Mary.

"Isn't it cool how they have managed to make and catch all their own food?" asked Maggie, with excitement.

"Yeah, I am really impressed. I couldn't believe how warm the cave was when I woke up," said Sarah.

"Me too. I am sure it is warmer than my room back home," said Maggie, laughing.
Sarah laughed too, nodding her head in agreement.

"What's the plan for today?" asked Sarah.

"Well, Rick and I were talking about learning more of what the children do here but Sophia has asked us to teach the small children to talk and read, if we can," answered Maggie.

"Awesome. That will be exciting for everyone," said Sarah.

She liked the thought of spending time with the children and helping them to learn.

"What can I do to help?" asked Sarah, leaning forward to look at Mary.

"No, boys get eggs. Then we eat," said Mary.
She poured water into the powder and began mixing it with her hands. Once the powder had turned to a dough she made little balls. Then she flattened them and lay them on the hot

rocks around the fire. The dough made a sizzling noise. Maggie and Sarah watched as it turned brown. Mary moved forward, using her hands, she carefully picked the bread up and turned it over. It was golden brown and hard on the one side. After a few minutes she lifted the bread off the rocks and placed it on a woven mat beside her. She did the same with the remaining balls until they were all cooked. Sarah jumped up and walked over to their crates. She took out two tins of baked beans and the tin opener. Sitting down beside Maggie, she opened the tins and stood them near the hot rocks to warm.

"What this?" asked Baby, coming to sit down next to Sarah.

"Those are baked beans. Yummy," she said, rubbing her tummy.
Baby giggled and stared at the two tins, then licked her lips.

"Me eat?" she asked.

"Yes, we can all have some with breakfast," said Sarah.
Baby looked confused.

"What bekfist?" said Baby.

"Um, it's the name for the meal you eat in the morning," answered Sarah.

"Oh," said Baby, though she still looked unsure.

Franklin, Peter and Cliff arrived just then, Cliff was carrying a basket of eggs. He handed it to Charlotte. She knelt down next to a flat, hot rock and cracked one onto the rock. The egg bubbled and hardened. Once it was cooked she removed it and put it onto another woven mat. Charlotte did the same with the next egg until all the eggs had been cooked. Tim walked around checking on everyone. When Charlotte had finished the last egg, he let out a whistle and the children all gathered together in a circle on the sandy ground. Mary placed the bread in the centre and Charlotte put the eggs down. Sarah fetched the baked beans and put them with the rest of the food. She looked around and realized they didn't have any plates so she ran over to the crates and collected all the plates, spoons and forks that she could find. She took them to the circle of children and handed one to each child. Using her spoon she placed baked beans on each plate. The children watched in amazement. Thumb used his hands to pick up a bean and put it in his mouth.

"Ummm, nice," he shouted, happily.

The other children giggled and then tried their own. Noises of delight could be heard from all of them as they scooped the beans into their mouths and tasted them. Rick, Maggie and Sarah just watched, smiling at how happy they had made the children.

Mary handed out the bread and eggs. Everyone sat quietly eating. When the meal was done everyone got up and began to clear away without being asked. It was like each person had their own task and knew what needed to be done. Sarah was impressed with the little system they had going. They worked like a real family.

Over the next two days Sarah, Maggie and Rick worked with the children, helping them with their tasks and teaching them new tricks. Sarah helped the little children to talk and read while Maggie went with the bigger girls to collect food and set new traps. They filled water bottles with fresh water and took it all back to the cave.

Rick went up each day with the bigger boys to load the hot rocks from the top of the volcano. They chopped trees for firewood and cut down leaves for weaving. It was a glorious two days as the children all worked side by side. As the time passed Sarah, Rick and Maggie taught the bigger children how to talk correctly and all about the rest of the world. Tim, especially, listened with eagerness, asking lots of questions until he understood.

"Where your boat?" asked Tim.

"Where is your boat," corrected Rick.
Tim tried again.

"Where is your boat?"

"We set anchor, just off the coast, near our camp," said Rick. "Would you like to see it?"

"Ooo, yes me would," said Tim.

"You mean, 'Yes, I would'," corrected Rick.

"Yes, I would," said Tim, smiling at the sound of his own voice.
Rick smiled back at him.

"Sure. We can go and see it tomorrow, if you like?" replied Rick.
Tim shook his head, up and down, wildly. His eyes lit up with excitement.

"We all go?" He stopped. "Can we all go?" Tim corrected himself.

"Well done. Yes, we can all go," said Rick.
When everyone was sitting around the fire that night Tim stood up and whistled. Everyone stopped talking and turned to listen.

"Tomorrow, we can all go to the boat," he said, proudly.

The children cheered. Sarah and Maggie looked at each other, impressed with how well Tim had spoken.

That night Sarah and Maggie lay in their sleeping bags, alongside each other, chatting.

"I miss home, Maggie," said Sarah, sadly.

"Me too. I love being here with the children, but I also want to see my family again," said Maggie.

"What are we going to do? We can't just leave them here," whispered Sarah.

"They could come back in the boat with us. Maybe we can find someone, who can help us to find their families," whispered Maggie, back.

"That would be awesome," said Sarah, a little too loudly.

"What are you girls talking about?" asked Rick.

"Come here," called Maggie, to her brother. Rick got up and went over to where the girls were lying.

"We think..." Said Sarah.

"Let's take..." said Maggie at the same time.

"One at a time please," said Rick, putting up his hands to slow them down.

"What if we took the kids back on the boat with us. We could help them find their families," said Maggie.

"I have been thinking about that myself actually, but that's if they want to go. They have a life here and they don't know anything else," replied Rick.

"True," said Sarah, sadly.

"But we can't just leave them and I want to go home," moaned Maggie.

"Give me a few more days. I will talk to Tim and see how he feels about it. Okay?" said Rick.

"Okay," said the girls, together.
Sarah and Maggie woke, the following morning, at the same time. It was hard to sleep once the noise from the boulder being rolled open, at the entrance to the cave, sounded, down the long tunnel. There seemed to be a buzz of excitement all around. Everyone was busy doing something, dashing from one corner of the cave to the other.
When Boy saw the girls were awake, he ran over to them. He pulled on Maggie's arm.

"Up, up. You must get up. We go boat today," said Boy.

"Ah, yes. That's why everyone is so excited," said Maggie, getting up.
Sarah also got up and they walked to the centre of the cave. Breakfast was already done. The three small children ran towards them, grabbed their hands and led them to the circle, where they all sat down, on the ground. The food was placed in the centre and everyone waited eagerly for Mary to pass it around. Sarah noticed everyone eating faster than usual.

"Wow, is everyone excited about going to the boat today?" she asked, even though she knew the answer.
Nobody said a word. They all just kept eating, shaking their heads up and down.

"Okay then. Let's clean up and go," said Rick, loudly.
Any food that was uneaten was shoved into mouths. The kids jumped up and ran around clearing the breakfast stuff away.
Rick went over to the crates and collected their three bags. He checked there was water in each bottle, some of their snack bars, fruit and bread that Mary had made for the trip. The other boys helped to carry extra water. Sarah, Maggie and Rick placed their hats on their

heads. Thumb looked up at Rick then ran off. He returned with a softly woven mat, placed it on his head and used a weaved rope to tie it down. Rick laughed.

"Clever thinking Thumb," said Rick, putting out his hand for a high five.

Rick had taught the boys the difference between a hand shake and a high five. Thumb jumped up and slapped Rick's hand.

"High five," he shouted.

"High five, mate," said Rick with a broad grin.

All the kids scrambled off to find their own mat and rope. Soon everyone was wearing a woven hat.

"Right, are we ready to go?" asked Rick.

"Yes," came a chorus of voices.

"Let's go," said Tim.

11
BOY OVER BOARD

Everyone filed out of the cave in a straight line, almost from biggest to smallest.

The children walked along the volcano, crossed the stream and headed down the hill. Passed the waterfall and into the forest. Soon they were on the beach and Rick led them around the sandy strip, until they came to the spot from where the boat could be seen. Rick stopped and pointed. The children stared in amazement. Their mouths hung open with surprise. They had never seen a boat before. Even Tim could barely remember what a boat looked like, as he was much younger when they had arrived on the island.

Rick walked over to the row boat, that was tied to a nearby tree. He loosened the rope. The boys helped him to push it into the water and then got in.

"We will go to the boat and then I'll come back for you," said Rick, to the girls and the smaller children.

The little ones moaned at the thought of being left behind.

"I will be back soon," said Rick, ruffling Thumbs hair.

Rick climbed in and passed an ore to Tim.

"You will need to sit there," said Rick.

He pointed to the opposite side of the small boat. Tim sat down, holding the ore straight up, in the air, unsure of what to do with the object he had been given.

Rick sat down on his side of the boat. Maggie and Sarah gave them a push and the little boat moved slowly into deeper water. The tide was low and Rick could use his ore, on the sand, to push them out further into the water. Tim soon figured out what Rick was doing with the ore and did the same. As the water got deeper Rick began to paddle. Tim followed. Soon they were heading out towards the boat. Everyone else watched in silence from the shore. The little boat got smaller and smaller until it was just a speck in the ocean. Sarah and Maggie could make out the little bodies as they climbed aboard the large boat, but it was still a long wait before they saw Rick climb back into the rowing boat and head towards them again. Finally, Rick floated back onto the sand. Thumb nearly knocked Baby over, in his excitement to get to the boat. Sarah just laughed and helped her up. They lifted Boy and Baby into the boat and then helped the rest of the girls in. Once everyone was seated, Sarah and Maggie gave the little boat another nudge and then jumped in too. Maggie grabbed the other ore and helped Rick to get the boat out to deeper water.

It seemed to take forever to reach the boat but finally they made it. Rick helped the girls up and then the smaller children were handed to the bigger girls. Once everyone was on board, Rick climbed up and onto the boat. Tim was sitting on the captain's chair, pretending to steer the boat. Cliff and Henry were looking at all the knobs and buttons on the consol. Ben; Franklin and Peter were hanging over the back of the boat. They were in deep debate over the propellers, that hung just below the surface of the water.

Maggie took the other girls below deck to show them the sleeping quarters; kitchen and store room. Sarah stayed on deck to keep an eye on the three little children, who seemed to be everywhere at once. Sarah found herself running from one to the other, trying to stop them from doing crazy stuff, like hanging over the railing, to look into the water.

On the upper deck, Rick had started the engine. Everyone cheered, as the roar from the motor filled the air. Baby grabbed her ears and started to cry. Sarah went to her, knelt down and gave her a cuddle.

"It's okay, Baby. That's just Rick starting the boat," said Sarah, pointing up at the boys on the upper deck. However, in that same moment, in the excitement, Cliff bumped the throttle and the boat jerked forward, into motion. Peter, who was leaning over the end of the boat, to see the propellers spinning wildly, fell overboard.

There was sudden chaos. Franklin and Ben started shouting for help. Sarah turned to see what the commotion was all about and realized someone was missing. Just then, Maggie appeared from below.

"Maggie, someone has fallen overboard," shouted Sarah.

Maggie dashed to the back of the boat, while Sarah ran to the upper deck.

"Rick, cut the engines. Someone has fallen off the boat," yelled Sarah, as she ran up the three steps to Rick.

Rick spun around, his face went white with shock. He hit the off button and the roar of the engine died immediately.

In the meantime Maggie had jumped into the water to help Peter. She struggled to keep him above the small waves that had been created by the propellers. Rick jumped off the upper deck and ran to the other side of the boat. Without stopping, he grabbed the life buoy and dived into the water after his sister.

Everyone was now standing at the end of the boat watching the three children struggling in the water. Fortunately, both Maggie and Rick were strong swimmers. Rick was holding Peter under the arms, while Peter, desperately, clung to the life buoy. Maggie swam back to the boat and lifted herself onto the ledge. Once Rick had reached her, she helped to lift Peter out of the water. He coughed and spluttered, trying to clear his throat of all the water he had swallowed. Maggie helped her brother up and they both sat on the ledge, breathing deeply.

"Wow, that was intense," said Rick, breathlessly.

"I thought he was going to drown me," said Maggie, with a shaky voice.

Rick put his arm around his sister and gave her a squeeze.

"You were very brave just diving in there," he said.

"Are you okay?" asked Sarah, coming up behind them.

"Yeah, we are fine. How is Peter?" asked Rick.

"He'll be fine. I think he is in shock. He is just sitting there shaking," said Sarah.

"The poor guy must have got the fright of his life," said Rick, getting up to check on Peter. Maggie got to her feet too and followed Rick. Sarah had covered Peter with a towel and he sat quietly on the bench. Everyone was fussing around him.

"Hey mate. You okay?" asked Rick, placing his hand on Peter's shoulder.

Peter just shook his head up and down.

"Well, I think that is enough excitement for one day. Should we start making our way back to land?" asked Rick.

"Ahhh," said Thumb.

"I want to stay on boat."

"We could just have our lunch and then go back?" said Maggie, giving her brother a pleading glance.

"Okay. Good idea, Maggie. I am starving, come to think of it," said Rick, winking at her. Maggie grinned.

"Who's hungry?" she said.

"Me," everyone called out.

Mary shuffled around getting the food ready. Sophia and Charlotte helped to lay a large blanket out on the deck. Once everything was ready the children sat down in their circle and Mary handed out the food. Meal times were always quiet as everyone chewed away, happily, lost in thought.

12
MONKEY BUSINESS

The trip home went smoothly. Once everyone was back on the beach, they formed a queue and walked quietly through the forest They past the waterfall, went along the volcano and back to the cave. Mary; Sophia, Maggie and Sarah stopped to collect fresh water in the water bottles and then made their way back to the cave.

When they arrived back, the usual routine began. The boys headed up the mountain to gather the rocks, while the girls were left to collect the food.

The boys had barely made it half way up the volcano, when they heard the noise. They could hear the girls screaming and someone was crying loudly. The different noises were confusing. Without wasting time, the boys sprinted down the hill, towards the noise. It was coming from within the forest. Tim and Rick were the fastest and managed to get to the heart of the noise, first.

They could not believe their eyes. More than ten monkeys were darting around. Mary was lying on the ground. Sophia and Charlotte were fighting with a large monkey, over a weaved basket. Maggie was swinging her basket around trying to keep the monkeys away.

From one of the bushes, a monkey was screeching and shaking the branches around.
Rick grabbed Maggie's arm, to avoid being hit with the basket.

"What's going on?" shouted Rick.

"One of the baby monkeys got caught in the trap and the mother is trying to free it but the other monkeys attacked us when we tried to get closer. I think Mary has hurt her leg," yelled Maggie, above the loud cries.

"Check the cave," shouted Tim, to the other boys.

Then he ran to Mary and bent over her, to protect her from the monkeys. After checking her leg, he scooped her up in his arms, turned and ran towards the cave.

Rick ran at the monkeys still holding onto the basket, yelling loudly. The monkeys let out screeching cries but dropped the basket and darted back into the trees. He grabbed Sophia and Charlotte by the hand and pulled them away, in the direction of the cave.

"Maggie, get out of there," yelled Rick.

Maggie turned and ran behind them, leaving her basket on the ground.

As they approached the cave, Tim was waiting at the entrance. Once they were all in, he rolled the large boulder across the opening to keep the monkeys out. Exhausted, he leaned his back against the rock and breathed a sigh of relief.

"Is everyone okay?" asked Tim.
Rick was bent over, trying to catch his breath. He nodded and gestured towards the girls. Everyone nodded.

"We're fine," said Chalet.
Sarah came running down the dark tunnel.

"I heard the screaming. Is someone hurt?" asked Sarah.

"I think Mary has hurt her leg but otherwise, we are fine," said Maggie.
Sarah went over to Mary. She had a few cuts down the one side of her leg.

"I'll get a bandage, but it doesn't look too bad," said Sarah, comforting Mary.
Mary gave her a smile.

"Thank you," she said.
Sarah disappeared into the tunnel.
Just then more screams sounded from the inside of the cave. Tim and Rick bolted away like runners at a starting line. They arrived at the main centre of the cave to find monkeys climbing down the ropes, that hung from the top of the volcano.

"Everyone get out. Run. Now," shouted Tim.

Rick grabbed Thumb and Baby around the waist, tucking them under each of his arms and ran. Ben grabbed Boy, while Franklin grabbed Sarah's hand and pulled her towards the entrance of the cave. He was running so fast that Sarah almost lost her footing a few times.

Hendry and Cliff, running backwards, hurled rocks at the monkeys as they descended into the volcano.

"Help me roll the stone away," shouted Tim, to Rick as they reached the entrance.

Rick put the small children down and ran over to help Tim.

As soon as the boulder was pushed aside, children ran out in every direction.

"This way," yelled Tim, trying to keep everyone together.

"Sarah, take them," said Tim, pointing at Thumb and Boy.

"Mary, you take Baby. Come on. Run," he yelled.

The girls grabbed the children by the hand and Sarah sprinted out in front. Mary followed, with the rest of the children running behind her.

The boys were picking up sticks and rocks, as they ran. Flinging them at the charging monkeys to keep them back.
Sarah ran as fast as she could, almost dragging the boys behind her.
Tim looked up and realized Sarah was running in the wrong direction.

"Sarah's running to the cliff. Stop her," shouted Tim.

"STOP!" screamed Rick and Tim, at the same time.
Sarah glanced back to see who they were shouting at. Tim was looking at her, but she kept running.

"There's a cliff. STOP," he yelled.
Sarah stopped suddenly.

She looked down, in a daze.

"Stop, Sarah, you are jumping too high," wailed Mikey.
Sarah stopped jumping and flopped onto her bottom, on the trampoline.

"Sorry, I was running from the monkeys," she said.

"What monkeys?" asked Chris, with a puzzled look on his face.

She tugged at her brothers and sat them down beside her.

"Well," she whispered, leaning in for effect. "Just imagine…"

The Imagine Series

Here are the three winning pictures from Book #1, The Play Centre Adventure – Well done!

Cleo, 8

Mia, 9

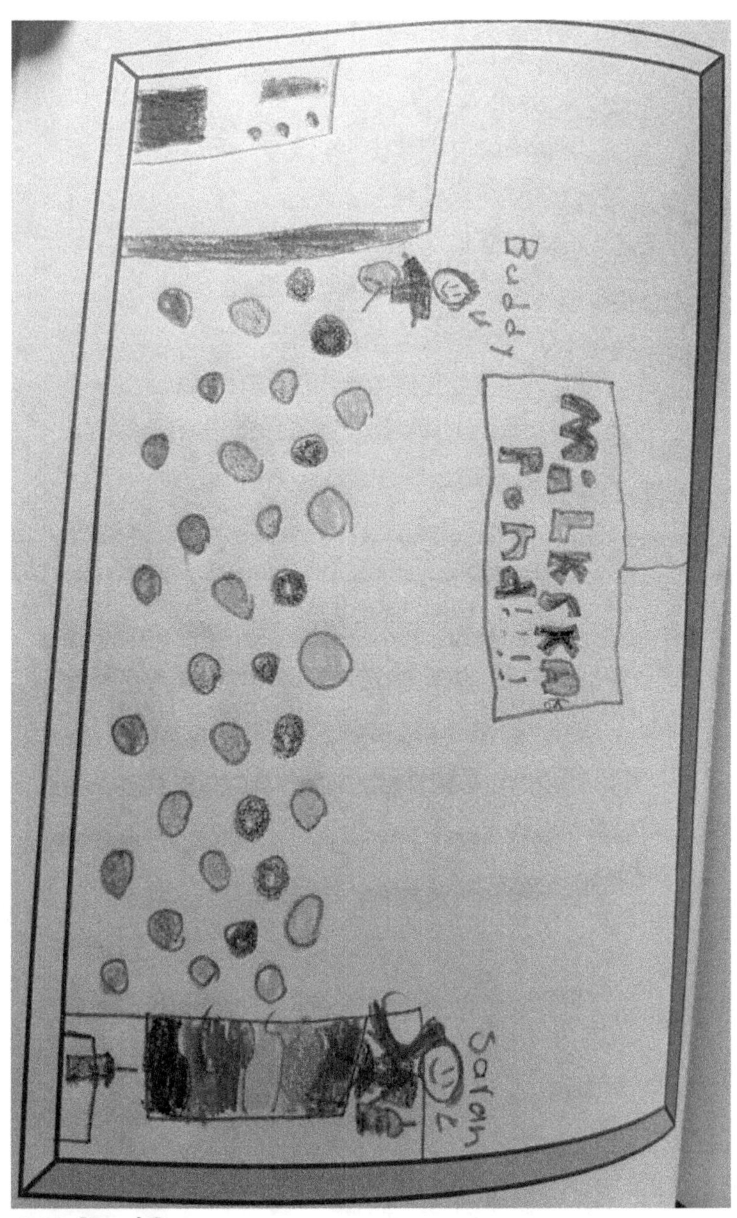

ANayKa, 10

ABOUT THE AUTHOR:
LARA HUNTER

I love to write and have done since I was a young girl. Now, I have my own little girl and she is the inspiration for my books. It was her amazing imagination that encouraged me to begin the Imagine series. While I love composing the stories, I also love to give you, the reader, the opportunity to be involved. Writing can sometimes be a lonely job to do – knowing that you get to be a part of this journey with me, makes my writing even more exciting. My goal is to complete five books within the series. I hope you enjoy each one of them. Please remember to send me your pictures and missing chapter from book 1 & 2 so I can enjoy your experience, with you.

www.ingramcontent.com/pod-product-compliance
Lightning Source LLC
Chambersburg PA
CBHW061520050726

47593CB00002B/656